SHIPMENT 1

Wed in Wyoming by Allison Leigh
Do You Take This Maverick? by Marie Ferrarella
A Conard County Baby by Rachel Lee
A Randall Hero by Judy Christenberry
The Texas Wildcatter's Baby by Cathy Gillen Thacker
The Bull Rider's Son by Cathy McDavid

SHIPMENT 2

The Cowboy's Valentine by Donna Alward
Most Eligible Sheriff by Cathy McDavid
The Lawman Lassoes a Family by Rachel Lee
A Weaver Baby by Allison Leigh
The Last Single Maverick by Christine Rimmer
A Montana Cowboy by Rebecca Winters

SHIPMENT 3

Trust a Cowboy by Judy Christenberry
Million-Dollar Maverick by Christine Rimmer
Sarah and the Sheriff by Allison Leigh
The Cowboy's Homecoming by Donna Alward
A Husband in Wyoming by Lynnette Kent
The Comeback Cowboy by Cathy McDavid
The Rancher Who Took Her In by Teresa Southwick

SHIPMENT 4

A Cowboy's Promise by Marin Thomas
The New Cowboy by Rebecca Winters
Aiming for the Cowboy by Mary Leo
Daddy Wore Spurs by Stella Bagwell
Her Cowboy Dilemma by C.J. Carmichael
The Accidental Sheriff by Cathy McDavid

SHIPMENT 5

Bet on a Cowboy by Julie Benson
A Second Chance at Crimson Ranch by Michelle Major
The Wyoming Cowboy by Rebecca Winters
Maverick for Hire by Leanne Banks
The Cowboy's Second Chance by Christyne Butler
Waiting for Baby by Cathy McDavid

SHIPMENT 6

Colorado Cowboy by C.C. Coburn
Her Favorite Cowboy by Mary Leo
A Match Made in Montana by Joanna Sims
Ranger Daddy by Rebecca Winters
The Baby Truth by Stella Bagwell
The Last-Chance Maverick by Christyne Butler

SHIPMENT 7

The Sheriff and the Baby by C.C. Coburn
Claiming the Rancher's Heart by Cindy Kirk
More Than a Cowboy by Cathy McDavid
The Bachelor Ranger by Rebecca Winters
The Cowboy's Return by Susan Crosby
The Cowboy's Lady by Nicole Foster

SHIPMENT 8

Promise from a Cowboy by C.J. Carmichael
A Family, At Last by Susan Crosby
Romancing the Cowboy by Judy Duarte
From City Girl to Rancher's Wife by Ami Weaver
Her Holiday Rancher by Cathy McDavid
An Officer and a Maverick by Teresa Southwick
The Cowboy and the CEO by Christine Wenger

SARAH AND THE SHERIFF

NEW YORK TIMES BESTSELLING AUTHOR

ALLISON LEIGH

Recycling programs for this product may not exist in your area.

HARLEQUIN® WESTERN HEARTS

ISBN-13: 978-1-335-50772-3

Sarah and the Sheriff
First published in 2007.
This edition published in 2020.

This edition published by arrangement with Harlequin Books S.A.

For questions and comments about the quality of this book, please contact us at CustomerService@Harlequin.com.

Harlequin Enterprises ULC
22 Adelaide St. West, 40th Floor
Toronto, Ontario M5H 4E3, Canada
www.Harlequin.com

Printed in U.S.A.

Though her name is frequently on bestseller lists, **Allison Leigh**'s high point as a writer is hearing from readers that they laughed, cried or lost sleep while reading her books. She credits her family with great patience for the time she's parked at her computer, and for blessing her with the kind of love she wants her readers to share with the characters living in the pages of her books. Contact her at allisonleigh.com.

For my parents,
who've celebrated more than
forty-nine years together.
You are my inspiration.

Prologue

She hadn't thought things could get any worse.

Twenty-one years old.

Pregnant with no husband in the wings. No fiancé, of course. And a boyfriend? Oh, please.

Sarah wanted to laugh over that one, and might have if she hadn't felt so horrible.

Laughing might have drawn attention to herself, anyway. And attention was the last thing she wanted, considering she was practically hiding in the thick of an oleander bush that was as tall as she was.

She brushed at the pink blossoms tickling her arm, shifting her position. The bride was handing off her spray of deep red roses to her attendant and Sarah nearly jumped out of her skin when a voice spoke behind her.

"I love weddings."

She looked at the small, wizened woman who'd toddled up beside her. If she'd noticed anything odd about Sarah's position, virtually hiding in a bush, she said nothing. "Don't you, dear?"

Feeling stupid—nothing new there, either—Sarah managed a shrug and a noncommittal smile.

Again, the woman didn't seem to take any notice. She just peered around the bushes of the Malibu garden in which they stood, toward the bridal couple standing about fifty yards away. "They have weddings at this spot pretty regularly. I can certainly understand why, though, with the Pacific Ocean in the background and the garden here. It's a lovely setting."

"Mmm-hmm."

"Of course, in my day—" the woman's voice dropped, confidentially "—choosing to get married out of doors usually meant the bride was going to be having an early baby. Premature, but not really premature." Her face wrinkled even more as she continued her study. "Times are different nowadays. And the bride obviously has already *had* her baby. Looks like a tiny mite, being held like that against the daddy's shoulder. Wonder if it is a boy or a girl?"

Sarah couldn't manage even a shrug. "Boy." The word felt raw against her throat. The reality of that boy baby had felt raw in her soul since she'd learned of his existence a few weeks earlier. "And not so tiny. He's nearly nine months old already."

"Really? You know the couple? Why aren't you sitting with the rest of the guests?"

Sarah wished she'd kept quiet. "I didn't expect to make the wedding," she murmured.

"Are you a friend of the bride or the groom?"

"Groom," she said. "Acquaintances." Which was a lie.

One didn't make love with acquaintances.

They didn't fool themselves into thinking they loved an acquaintance.

The explanation was good enough for the woman, though. "Ahh. Well, that baby will probably grow up as handsome as his daddy there," the woman mused. "My husband was tall and dark like that. Italian." Her wrinkles deepened again with a surprisingly impish smile. "Passionate."

Sarah forced her lips to curve.

"Bride's gown is pretty, too. Nothing I'd

want to see my granddaughter wearing, mind you, but still pretty."

The gown *was* pretty. Sophisticated. Sleeveless and reaching just past her knees. It wasn't even white, but a sort of pinkish oyster-like hue that seemed to reflect the glow of the sun as it hung on the horizon over the ocean.

"What do you do, dear?"

Sarah swallowed. "I'm an intern at the L.A. office of Frowley-Hughes."

The woman looked blank.

"It's a brokerage firm."

"Ahh. Financial stuff." Seemingly satisfied, the woman turned her focus back to the wedding party. "I taught school. Until my own children started coming along."

Sarah managed not to press her hand against her abdomen. She knew it was still flat beneath her T-shirt and jeans, but she was painfully aware that state would end soon enough. "How many did you have?"

"Four. And now I have eleven grandchildren. They're scattered all over, though. Don't come out to see their old grandma here in California too often."

Sarah felt a swift longing. "My family is mostly in Wyoming."

"Long way from here."

"Yes." Her gaze settled on the groom once more. "A long way."

"Maybe someday you'll have a beachside wedding. You'd be a beautiful bride. Such wonderful long hair you have."

Sarah's throat tightened. The memory of his hands tangling in her hair taunted her. "Thank you. But I don't have any plans to get married."

The woman smiled and waved her hand. "Forgive me, but you're just young. You wait. You'll want a husband and children at some point. I can tell. Oh, look." She nodded toward the wedding party again. "They're doing the rings now. Such a beautiful couple," she said again, her voice a satisfied sigh.

The bride did look beautiful.

The groom did look handsome.

And the baby—well, the baby was a baby. Sarah couldn't blame a baby.

She couldn't blame that lovely bride, either.

But the groom?

Oh, she could certainly blame him, all right.

But the person she blamed the most?

That would be herself.

She turned away, pushing the oleander branches out of her way, being careful not to let them snap back and hit the other woman.

"Don't you want to watch the rest of the wedding?"

Sarah shook her head gently. "No. I've seen enough."

More than enough.

Only problem was, she'd seen it all too late. Much too late.

And though Sarah had thought things couldn't get any worse, it was only a matter of months before she learned that they *could.*

Chapter 1

The first time Sarah saw the name on her class roster, she felt shock unlike anything she'd felt in years roll through her.

Elijah Scalise.

Not that daunting of a name, really. It surely suited the dark-haired eight-year-old boy who'd soon be joining her third-grade class. She had made a point of not looking at the boy's picture, even though she was perfectly aware that there was one. It was framed in a plain gold frame that sat on his grandmother's desk in the classroom right next to Sarah's classroom. Genna Scalise often talked about her grandson, Eli.

Sarah hadn't expected to ever be the boy's teacher, though.

She set aside the roster on her desk and went to the window that overlooked the playground. Frost still clung to the exterior corners and she could feel the coolness of the pane radiating from it. Outside, the bell hadn't yet rung and children were clambering over the swings and jungle gym. Winter scarves flew in the breeze and boots crunched over the crispy skiff of snow scattered across the playground.

Despite the cold, they were enjoying the last few minutes of freedom before they had to settle down into their seats. Until they broke for recess in a few hours, that was.

Nothing like feeling carefree.

She couldn't remember the last time she'd felt as carefree as they looked.

Which wasn't strictly true. She could probably pick the exact date on the calendar when she'd stopped feeling carefree.

Her gaze slid to the class roster.

"So, why didn't you tell me the news?" The chipper female voice drew her attention to the doorway of her classroom.

"Hey, Dee. What news?"

"About the new deputy." Deirdre Crowder was the sixth-grade teacher and at five-foot-nothing, she was about as big as a minute. Her blue eyes were mischievous. "He works for *your* uncle, girl, but you could have shared the wealth. A new, single man suddenly in town and all that. If it were the week before Christmas rather than Thanksgiving, I'd consider him to be our very own Christmas present!"

Sarah now had years of practice under her belt at keeping her true thoughts to herself. "Go for it," she said with a smile. "He's my new student's father. And you know I don't get involved with my kids' fathers."

Dee's eyebrows lifted as she sauntered into the room. Her shoulder-length blond hair seemed to crackle with the energy that kept it curled in loose ringlets. "I may have only come to Weaver a year ago, but as far as I can tell, you don't get *involved* with anyone. What's with you?" She joined Sarah at the window. "If I had your looks I'd be dating every available man in town."

"There is nothing wrong with your looks," Sarah countered. She'd heard Dee's opinion plenty in the months since school had begun in August. "Deputy Tommy Potter thinks they're about perfect."

"Oh, Tommy." Dee shook her head, dismissively. "Unless he was going to arrest me for something, or wants to spread a little gossip, that boy moves about as slow as molasses in winter. He has no gumption." She pushed up the sleeves of her bright red sweater and pointed out the window. "Since it might as well be winter, with all that snow on the ground, you can just imagine the snail's pace I'm talking about."

Sarah's lips curved. "You're the one who moved to a small town, Dee. Could have stayed in Cheyenne where the pickings were more varied."

Dee pressed her nose against the cold windowpane, looking not much older than the children playing outside. "Have you met him? The new deputy, I mean? I heard he comes from Weaver."

If Sarah hadn't been prepared to see that name on her class roster, she definitely wasn't prepared to discuss her new student's father. "He left Weaver a long time ago."

"Yeah, but you *did* know him, right? Most everyone in Weaver seems to know everyone else."

"Maybe by sight," Sarah allowed. Though the Clay family had its history with the Scalise family—history that had nothing to do with her experience with him. "Talk to Genna," she suggested. "She's his mother. She could tell you everything you ever wanted to know about Max."

Her throat tightened.

Max.

At the mention of Genna, the most senior teacher at Weaver Elementary, Dee turned her back on the window. "How's she healing up, anyway?"

"Fine, last I heard." Sarah felt a little guilty that she didn't know more. That she hadn't made a more concerted effort to visit Genna herself. After all, they were coworkers and had been since Sarah began teaching at Weaver Elementary nearly six years ago. Genna was a friend of her mother's. Her aunts!

"What was she doing skiing at her age, anyway? It's no wonder she broke some bones."

"Anyone can have a skiing accident, even someone who's barely twenty-five," Sarah said pointedly.

Dee grinned impishly and rolled her eyes. But Sarah was spared her comment when the bell rang, sharp and shrill.

"To the salt mine," Dee said, heading for the classroom door. "Want to head over to Classic Charms one night this week? See if Tara's got anything new in?"

Sarah nodded. The children outside had scattered like leaves on the wind when the bell rang, and now she could hear footsteps ringing on the tile floor in the corridor. "Sure."

Classic Charms was the newest shop to open its doors in Weaver, though it had eschewed the new shopping center area for a location right on Main Street.

Dee swiveled, deftly avoiding a collision with the first trio of kids bolting into Sarah's classroom.

Sarah began passing out the workbooks she'd corrected over the weekend as the tables slowly filled. She had seventeen kids in her class this year.

Correction.

Eighteen, now.

They sat two to a table, usually, though she had enough room for them to all sit separately if need be. Some years were like that. This year though, had so far been peaceful.

"Thanks, Miz Clay." Bright-eyed Chrissy Tanner beamed up at her as she accepted her workbook. "Are we having science today?"

"It's Monday, isn't it?" she asked lightly and continued passing through the room. Her attention, though, kept straying to the door.

Sooner or later, Eli would be there. Her

gaze flicked to the wide-faced clock affixed high on the wall and noted he'd have three minutes before he'd be tardy. Not that she'd enforce that rule with a brand-new student on his very first day. She wasn't *that* much a stickler for the rules.

The thought struck her as incredibly ironic.

The last workbook delivered, she walked back through the tables, heading to the front of the classroom where she picked up her chalk and finished writing out the day's lesson plan on the blackboard. The sound of chatter and laughter and scraping chairs filled the room.

It was familiar and normal.

Ordinarily those sounds, this classroom, felt safe to Sarah.

But not today.

Would *he* bring Eli?

Between her fingers, the chalk snapped into pieces. Squelching an impatient sound, she picked them off the floor, and rapidly finished writing as the final bell rang.

No Eli Scalise.

As she'd done every morning at the beginning of the school day, she moved across the room and closed the door. Regardless of her feelings about her new student and his presence—or lack of it—she had a class to teach.

She turned back to her students, raising her voice enough to get everyone's attention. "How many of you saw the double-rainbow yesterday?"

A bunch of hands shot up into the air.

And the lessons of the day began.

"Why do I gotta go to school?"

"Because."

Eli sighed mightily. "But you said we were going to go back to California."

"Not for months yet."

"So?"

Max Scalise pulled open the passenger door of the SUV he'd been assigned by Sawyer Clay, the sheriff. They were already late, thanks to a conference call he'd had to take about a recent case of his. "In."

His son, Eli, made a face, but tossed his brown-bag lunch and dark blue backpack inside before climbing up on the seat.

"Fasten the belt."

The request earned Max another pulled face. He shut the door and headed around to the driver's side. As he went, his eyes automatically scanned the area around them.

But there was nothing out of the ordinary. Just bare-branched trees. Winter-dry lawns not quite covered by snow. A few houses lined neatly along the street, all of them closed up tight against the chill. Only one of them had smoke coming from the chimney—his mother's house that they'd just left.

Genna was as comfortably situated as she could get in the family room, where Max had lit the fire in the fireplace as she'd requested. She had her heavy cast propped on pillows, a stack of magazines, a pot of her favorite tea, the television remote and a cordless phone.

Outside the houses, though, there were no particular signs of life.

His breath puffed out around his head in white rings and cold air snuck beneath the collar of his dark brown departmental jacket.

God, he hated the cold.

He climbed in the truck.

"I could'a stayed in California with Grandma Helene," Eli continued the minute Max's rear hit the seat.

"What's wrong with your grandmother here?" He made a U-turn and headed down the short hop to Main Street.

Eli hunched his shoulders. The coat he wore was a little too big for him. Max had picked up the cold-weather gear on their way to the airport. There hadn't been a lot of time for fine fitting. "Nuthin'," his son muttered.

"But she always visited us out *there*. How come we gotta come here this time?"

"You happen to notice that big old cast on Grandma's leg?" Max drove past the station house and turned once again, onto the street leading to the school. It took all of three minutes, maybe, given the significant distance.

The closer they got to the brick building that hadn't changed a helluva lot since the days when Max had run the halls, the more morose Eli became. If his boy slouched any more in his seat, he'd hang himself on the seatbelt.

"Look at the bright side," Max said. "You won't be bored."

Eli's eyes—as dark blue as Jennifer's had been—rolled. "Rather be bored back home than bored in there." He jerked his chin toward the building.

Max pulled into the parking lot and stopped near the main entrance. "Don't roll your eyes." Donna, the school secretary, had told him when he'd faxed in the registration forms from California that the office was just inside the main front doors. A different location than he'd remembered from his days there.

"Do they have an after-school program?"

Eli was used to one in California—two supervised hours of sports and games that had never managed to produce completed homework the way it should have.

"No."

Eli heaved a sigh. "I *hate* it here."

Unfortunately, Max couldn't say much to change his son's opinion. Not when he remembered all too clearly feeling exactly the same way. He reached over and caught Eli behind the head, tousling his hair. "It's only for a few months. Until Grandma's all healed up and can go back to teaching school." By then, hopefully, Max would have finished the job *he'd* been assigned. But Max didn't tell Eli that. He wasn't about to tell anyone in Weaver what his true purpose was there.

Someone was funneling meth through Weaver. It was coming out of Arizona by way of Colorado and heading north after Weaver, even—occasionally—on a locally contracted semi. But only occasionally.

The transports seemed to be wide and varied and Max's job was to determine who was organizing the local hub.

It was a job he'd managed to avoid being assigned until his mom broke her leg two weeks earlier. She'd needed help. His boss had been putting on the pressure. So here they were. Father and son and neither one too thrilled about it.

"I'm already late, you know." Eli dragged his backpack over his shoulder. It rustled against his slick coat. "On my first day. The teacher'll probably be mad for the rest of the year."

"I seriously doubt it," Max drawled. His son had inherited his mother's dramatic streak, as well.

"Is it a lady? Or a man?"

"Who?"

Eli started to roll his eyes again, but stopped at a look from Max. "The teach. I liked Mr. Frederick. He was cool."

"I have no idea."

Eli made a sound. "You didn't *ask*?"

Max felt a pang of guilt. He'd been more preoccupied with this unexpected—and unappealing—assignment than with the identity of Eli's temporary teacher. Max had only had a few days to take care of the school paperwork, as it was. But Eli was right about one thing. They were late. Both of them.

The sheriff had expected Max at the station nearly thirty minutes ago.

Great way to start off, Scalise.

He caught Eli's jacket and nudged his son around the corner into the office when he spotted the sign.

A young woman he didn't recognize smiled at

them the moment they came into her view. "The new student," she said cheerfully. "Welcome."

Max heard the gritty sigh that came out of Eli and hoped he was the only one who heard it. He didn't need Eli having trouble at this school. He needed everything to go as smoothly as possible. With no distractions, Max could finish his investigation as quickly as possible, and they could get the hell back out of Dodge. As soon as his mother could get back in the classroom.

Weaver held no great memories for him.

He was just as anxious to leave it again as Eli was. Telling his boy that, though, was *not* going to happen.

"Deputy Scalise—" the girl at the desk had risen "—I'm Donna. It's nice to meet you in person. You, too, Eli. I'll just let Principal Gage know you're here."

"He already knows." A balding man approached from behind them, hand outstretched. "Max. Good to see you. Been a long time."

"Joe." He shook the principal's hand. "Still can't believe you're head honcho here." Joe Gage had been a hellion of the highest order back when they'd been kids. "Guess they don't hold a little thing like blowing up the science room against a man."

"Guess not. They made you a deputy, and you were in that room with me."

"Whoa, Dad." Eli sounded impressed.

The principal chuckled. "Come on. I'll take you down to Eli's class." He looked at the boy as they stepped into the corridor once more. "Miss Clay. You'll like her."

Max's boot heels scraped the hard floor. Clay. Another name from the past.

Well, why not?

The Clay family had plenty of members—seemed to him there'd been a teacher among them.

For a moment, he wished he'd been more inclined to listen to his mother's talk of Weaver over the years. But she knew his reasons for not wanting to hear about the town well enough. Weaver was where Max's father betrayed everyone they knew. It was where Tony Scalise had abandoned them. And on her visits to see him and Eli, she barely mentioned details about her life back home. Mostly because it generally led to an argument between them.

Max had wanted Genna to leave a long time ago. To join him in California.

For reasons that still escaped him, she'd been just as determined to stay.

The principal stopped in front of a closed

classroom door. Through the big square window that comprised the top half of the door, he could see the rows of tables—situated in a sort of half circle—all occupied by kids about Eli's size. At the head of the class, he caught a glimpse of the teacher. Slender as a reed, dressed in emerald green from head to toe. A little taller than average and definitely young, he noted. Her arms waved around her as she spun in a circle, almost as if she were acting out some play.

Max started to smile.

Then the teacher stopped, facing the door with its generous window head-on. Through the glass, her sky-blue eyes met his.

He felt the impact like a sucker punch to the kidneys.

He'd only known one woman with eyes that particular shade.

The principal pushed open the door. "Pardon the interruption, Miss Clay," he said, ushering Eli inside. "This is your new student, Eli Scalise. Eli, this is Miss Clay."

Max stood rooted to the floor outside the doorway.

Sarah.

She was no longer looking at him with those eyes that were as translucent as the Wyoming winter sky, but at Eli.

Her smile was warm. Slightly crooked. And it made Max wonder if he'd imagined the frigid way she'd looked at him through the window.

"Eli," she greeted. "Come on in. Take off your coat. Can't have you roasting to death on your first day here." She gestured at the line of coats hanging on pegs. "We do our roasting only on Wednesdays."

Eli shot Max a studiously bored look. But Max still saw the twitch of Eli's lips.

A good sign. Maybe he wouldn't have to worry about Eli, after all.

He looked back at Sarah again.

What the hell was she doing here? A teacher of all things. When they'd been involved—

He cut off the thought.

She gave him no more attention than she gave the principal as she showed Eli where to sit, and after assuring herself that he had the usual school supplies, she moved back to the front of the class. Without a glance their way, she picked up right where she'd left off. "Okay, so if the tornado is spinning to the right," she turned on her heels and the braid she'd woven her hair into swayed out from her spine.

Max started when Joe Gage headed out of the classroom and pulled the door closed, cutting off whatever else Professor Sarah was imparting. "She's a good teacher," Joe said. "Strict. But she really cares about her kids."

Max headed back up the corridor with Joe. "How long has she been here?"

"This will be her sixth year. So, Donna tells me you've already completed all the paperwork for Eli. You put your mom down as his caretaker? Is Genna up to that?"

He could have asked a dozen questions about Sarah Clay.

He asked none.

"Eli doesn't need a lot of care. He's pretty independent. He'll do as much taking care of her as she does him." He didn't like feeling as though he had to explain himself. "With the job I might not always be available. You know. If Eli got sick or something, my mother can make decisions about him."

"Fine, fine." Joe accepted the explanation without a qualm. "I'll be glad when Genna can make it back to work here. So, I know Eli lost his mother a year or so back. I'm sorry to hear it. Anything else in your personal life that he's dealing with that we might need to know?"

Max shrugged. "He's annoyed as hell that I took him out of his regular school to come here."

Joe smiled. "That's not too surprising." He

stopped outside the office. "Any questions *you* have?"

None that he intended to ask Joe Gage. He shook his head and stuck out his hand. "Good to see you again."

"Deputy." Donna waved at him from her desk. "The sheriff just called here looking for you."

Not surprising. "I'm on my way over to the station house."

"I'll let him know for you," she offered.

"Don't worry about Eli," Joe told him. "He's in good hands."

Sarah Clay's hands, Max thought, as he headed out to his SUV.

It might have been seven years, but he still remembered the feel of those particular hands.

He climbed in the truck, and started it up, only to notice the brown bag sitting on the floor. Eli's lunch.

Dammit.

He grabbed it and strode back inside, right on past the office, around two corners, to the third door. He knocked on the window.

Once again, inside the classroom, Sarah stopped and looked at him.

The glass protected him from the fallout of

that glacial look. He definitely hadn't imagined it, then.

She moved across the room and opened the door. "What is it, Deputy?"

He held up the lunch sack. "Eli forgot this."

Her eyes seemed to focus somewhere around his left ear. She snatched the bag from his fingers and turned away.

He started to say her name.

But the door closed in his face.

Chapter 2

By the end of the day, Sarah felt as if she'd been through the wringer. She didn't have to look hard for the reason why, either.

Not when he sat in the chair next to her desk, a sullen expression on his young face. The rest of the students had already been dismissed for the day.

She pushed aside the stack of papers on her desk and folded her hands together on the surface, leaning toward him. All day, she'd been searching for some physical resemblance between him and his father, and it annoyed her to no end.

Unlike Max, who was as dark as Lucifer, his son was blond-haired and blue-eyed and had the appearance of an angel. But he'd been an absolute terror.

Nevertheless, she was determined to keep her voice calm and friendly. "Eli, you've had a lot of changes in your life lately. And I know that starting at a new school can be difficult. Why don't you tell me what your days were like at your last school?"

"Better 'n here," he said.

She held back a sigh. She'd be phoning his last school as soon as possible. "Better how?"

"We had *real* desks, for one thing."

She looked at the tables. The only difference between a desk and the table was the storage, which was taken care of by cubbies that were affixed to each side of the table. "Do you prefer sitting at your own table?"

He lifted one shoulder, not answering.

"If you do, then all you have to do is say so. We both know that you won't be sitting next to Jonathan tomorrow."

"He's a tool." His expression indicated what a condemnation that was.

"He's a student in my class, the same as you are and doesn't deserve to be picked on all afternoon by anyone."

"I wasn't picking on him."

She lifted her eyebrows. "Really?"

"I don't care what he said."

"Actually, Jonathan didn't say anything. He didn't have to. Eli, I saw you poking at him. You were messing with his papers. You even hid his lunch from him. And then on the playground after lunch, you deliberately hit him with the ball. So, what gives?"

"He didn't dodge fast 'nuff or he wouldn't have got hit."

"This isn't the best way to start off here, you know."

"So call my dad and tell him that."

She had no desire whatsoever to speak to his father. Just seeing Max in person for a brief five minutes had been more than enough for her. "Let's make a deal, shall we? Tomorrow is a brand-new day. We'll all start fresh. *Or*, we can add your name to the list on the board." She gestured to the corner of the board where two other names were already written. "You know how that works. The first time, you get your name on the board. The second time, you get a check mark and a visit to the principal. If you get another check mark, you're out of my class." Something that had never once occurred, but it was the commonly accepted practice at her school.

Eli looked glum. "That was Mr. Frederick's rule, too."

"Mr. Frederick was your last teacher? Did you think that system was unfair?"

The boy lifted his shoulder again, not looking at her.

She propped her chin on her palm. "I want you to enjoy class, Eli. It's no fun for any of us if one of our class members is miserable. But the fact of it is, if you're caught trying to deliberately hurt another student, there's not going to be *anything* I can do to help you. Principal Gage has very clear rules about behavior. What you did on the playground today was wrong."

"The ball hardly hit him."

"Only because he wasn't standing still. And don't act as if you were playing a game of dodgeball, because I know you weren't."

His face scrunched up, like he'd swallowed something bitter. "Sorry," he mumbled.

"It's Jonathan who deserves the apology. You can use my phone here to call him, if you'd like."

His lips parted. "*Now*?"

She could almost have let herself be amused by his appalled expression. "No time like the present. And I'll bet that Jonathan is home by now since he lives just around the corner." She plopped the phone on the corner of her desk in front of Eli and pulled out the phone list. "Ready?"

Eli morosely picked up the phone and dialed the number that she recited.

Deciding to give him at least the illusion of some privacy, she rose and moved away from her desk, crossing the room to straighten the art supplies still scattered across the counter. The students had been painting Thanksgiving turkeys that afternoon.

Behind her, she heard Eli deliver his apology. Short. Brief. About what she'd expected.

But at least he'd offered it.

She hadn't been sure he would, given his mutinous attitude that afternoon.

She tapped the ends of her handful of paintbrushes on the counter, then dropped them into the canning jar where they fanned out like some arty bouquet. She turned around to face Eli and caught him surreptitiously swiping his cheek.

Tension and irritation drained out of her the same way it always did when it came to working with kids.

Evidently, Eli—son of Max Scalise or not—was no exception.

"Remember that tomorrow is a brand-new day," she said to him. "All fresh. Right?"

He didn't exactly jump up and down in agreement. But he didn't roll his eyes, either.

"Come on. I'll walk you out. Is—is your dad supposed to pick you up?"

He shook his head. "I gotta walk."

This time she didn't hold back the urge to smile slightly. He made walking sound like a fate worse than death. "To your grandmother's house?"

"To the station house."

"Well, that's even closer." She pushed a mammoth amount of papers and books into her oversized book bag and grabbed her own coat off the hook. "Have you met the sheriff yet?"

Eli shook his head.

"He's not too scary," Sarah confided. "He's my uncle."

At that, the boy looked slightly interested. He hitched his backpack over his shoulder and followed her into the hallway. "You got relatives here?"

"Lots and lots. Can't swing a cat without hitting a member of the Clay family."

"Gross. Who'd wanna swing a cat?"

She chuckled. "Well, nobody, I guess."

"*There* you are."

Her chuckle caught in her throat at the sight of Max standing in the middle of the corridor. His dark, slashing brows were drawn together over his eyes. They varied from brown to green, depending on his mood.

Currently, they looked green and far from happy.

She looked down at Eli beside her. "Guess you won't have to make that walk after all."

The corner of his lips turned down. "Think I was better off if I'd'a had to," he muttered.

She curled her fingers around the webbed strap of her book bag to keep from tousling his hair. Terror or not, there was something about the boy that got to her.

Not that most kids didn't, she hurriedly reminded herself.

"You're late," Max said. His voice hadn't changed. It was still deep. Still slightly abrupt. As if he spoke only because he had to.

"Only about ten minutes. He had some questions we needed to take care of," Sarah said, answering before Eli could. The boy shot her a surprised look that she ignored.

Max's eyes narrowed. He still had the longest lashes she'd ever seen on a man. Long and thick, and as darkly colored as the hair on his head. "What kind of questions?"

She decided to let Eli handle that one.

"About, uh, sports," he finally said.

Max looked suspicious. "Truck's in the

parking lot," he said after a moment. "Go wait for me."

Eli gave that little shrug of his and headed down the hall. "See ya tomorrow, Miz Clay."

"See you, Eli." Her hand was strangling the web strap. "Deputy." She barely looked at Max as she turned on her heel, intending to head out the other way. She could wend her way through the school to a different exit.

"Sarah—"

Every nerve she possessed tightened. She felt it from the prickling in her scalp to the curling in her toes. And though she would have liked to keep walking—no, she would have *loved* to keep walking—she stopped and looked at him over her shoulder.

After all, he *was* the parent of her newest student. She would have to deal with him on that level no matter what her personal feelings were.

"Yes?"

His lips compressed for a moment. "I... how are you?"

She didn't know what she might have expected him to say, but it definitely hadn't been that. "Busy," she said evenly. "Did you need to discuss something about Eli?"

"I'm sorry he was late this morning. It won't happen again."

"Okay." When it seemed as if he had nothing further to say, she started to turn again.

"I didn't expect to see you here."

Which meant she'd never been a hot topic of conversation between him and his mother, since she'd been working with Genna for some time now. "I can say the same thing about you."

She felt certain that she imagined the flicker in his eyes at that. Wishful thinking on her part that he might feel something, anything, about what had happened all those years ago. He'd made his feelings then perfectly clear, even though he'd never been perfectly clear about anything else.

And darnitall, that fact *still* stung even though she'd made herself believe that it was all water beneath the bridge.

She shifted the weight of her book bag to her other shoulder. "Coming down a little in the world, aren't you? From detective to deputy?"

"The job meets my needs for now."

She didn't want to know *what* his needs might be. "Then you have my congratulations." Her tone said the contrary, however. "Excuse me. I have things I need to do." She turned again and strode down the corridor, the click of her shoes sounding brisk and hollow.

Max's hands curled as he watched the

bounce of that long, thick braid as Sarah strode away from him.

He didn't make the mistake of speaking her name again.

She hated him.

Well, could he blame her?

When it came to Sarah Clay, he pretty much hated himself, too.

God, but he still couldn't believe she was here. In Weaver.

Aware that Eli was still waiting for him, he headed out to the SUV. His son was fiddling with the scanner when he climbed in the truck.

"She tell ya?" Eli sat back in his seat as Max reset the equipment.

Great. Tell me what? He started driving away from the school. "What do you think?"

His son heaved a sigh, obviously assuming the worst. "Figures. I was only kidding with the guy. How was I supposed to know his glasses would fly off like they did? At least they didn't break or nothing, though."

He gave his son a hard look, thinking he was glad Eli was more open than his teacher evidently was. "Did you apologize?"

"Yes. I used Miz Clay's phone in the classroom."

"Good. Don't do it again."

"How come you came to get me?"

"I told you. You were late. I was worried."

Eli rolled his eyes. "What for? This place is dinky. I mean, geez, Dad. There's not even a real mall!"

"Missing those afternoons you liked to spend shopping, is that it?"

His son snorted. They both knew that Eli loathed shopping. That was one trait he had gotten from Max.

He drove past the station where he'd go back on duty after Eli was settled with Genna. He drummed the steering wheel. "So, what's your teacher like?"

"Besides a rat fink?"

Max let out an impatient breath. "She didn't tell me anything, pal. You did that all on your own."

"Geez." Eli's head hit the back of the seat. He looked out the window. "She's all right, I guess." He was silent for a moment. "She kinda reminds me of Mom."

Max let that revelation finish rocking. Since Jen had died of cancer almost fourteen months earlier, Eli rarely mentioned her of his own volition. "In what way?"

"I dunno. What's for supper?"

"Grandma's cooking."

"I thought we were here to take care of *her*."

"We are. But she's pretty bored sitting around all day letting her broken leg heal. She's not used to that much inactivity."

"Can *we* go skiing sometime?"

Max wanted to tell his son they could. He didn't want Eli to be miserable the entire time they were in Weaver. "We'll see." Most everything would depend on how well the case went.

"Do ya even know how to ski?"

"Smart aleck. Yeah, I know."

"Well, you just lived in California all my life."

"All your life, bud. Not all of mine."

"What about horses? Can we go riding horses sometime?"

Max suppressed a grimace. He and horses had never particularly gotten along. "We'll see."

"Did you know Miz Clay?"

The question, innocence and curiosity combined, burned. "Yeah. I knew her."

"Did you, like, go to school with her?"

"No. She's a lot younger than me."

"Well, yeah. 'Cuz you're old and she's still pretty."

A bark of laughter came out of him. Miz Clay *was* still pretty. Beautiful, in fact; all that youthful dewiness she'd possessed at twenty-one had given way to the kind of timeless looks that would last all of her life.

"That's why I keep you around, Elijah. To keep me humble."

His son smiled faintly. "She says you can't swing a cat without hitting someone from her family. Was she your girlfriend?"

He pulled to a sudden stop in his mother's driveway and the tires skidded a few inches. He needed to get out the snowblower, and soon. "Just because she's female doesn't mean she was my girlfriend. I just told you. She's a lot younger than me."

"How much younger?"

God, give him patience. "I don't know. A lot." Liar.

"Five years?"

As if a paltry five years mattered. "Twelve."

"Geez. You *are* old. Not like Grandma old, but still—"

"Enough. I'm not so old that I can't beat your butt inside the house."

Eli grinned and set off at a run, his backpack swaying wildly from his narrow shoulders.

Max jogged along behind him. At least one thing had gone right that day. Eli was smiling.

Just before his son bolted up the front porch, Max put on the speed and flew past him to open the storm door first.

"Dad!"

He shrugged and went inside. "Wipe your

boots," he reminded. He pulled his radio off his belt and set it on the hall table and tossed his jacket on the coatrack. "Hey, Ma."

Genna Scalise was sixty years old and looked a good ten years less. Her hair was still dark, her face virtually unlined. And she was currently trying to poke one end of an unfolded wire hanger beneath the thigh-high edge of her cast. "Turn the heat off under the pasta."

"Don't poke yourself to death." He went into the kitchen and turned off the stove burner. The churning water in the pot immediately stopped bubbling. The second pot on the stove held his mother's homemade sauce. "Smells great, but I thought you said you were just going to throw together a casserole or something." He went back in the family room and took the hanger from her frustrated hands. "Here. Try this." He handed over the long-handled bamboo back scratcher that he'd picked up at the new supermarket on the far side of town.

Her eyes lit as if he'd just told her she was going to have a second grandchild. She threaded the long piece beneath the edge of her cast and tilted back her head, blissfully. "Oh, you're a good boy, Max."

Eli snickered.

"How was school?"

"I got homework," the boy said by way of answering her. "Vocabulary."

"Well, horrors." She smiled. "Get a start on it before we have dinner." She withdrew the scratcher and set it on the couch, then held up her arms to Max. "Help me up, honey, so I can finish that."

He lifted her slender form off the couch. From above, he could hear Eli moving around upstairs. Doing his homework, hopefully. "When you said you wanted to cook today, I didn't think you meant making homemade pasta."

"What other kind of pasta is there?" She patted his cheek and reached for her crutches.

He followed her slow progress back into the kitchen. He wasn't used to seeing his mother have to struggle; he didn't like it. But he knew she didn't want him constantly helping her, either, considering they'd already had a few skirmishes on that score since his and Eli's arrival a few days earlier. "Why didn't you tell me Sarah Clay would be Eli's teacher?"

Balancing herself, she sat down on the high stool that Max had put in the kitchen for her. She gave him a sidelong look. "I didn't think about it. I assumed that you knew. Is there something wrong with her? She's a fine teacher."

He shook his head. He was hardly going to tell his mother about it.

She sighed and set down her long wooden spoon. "What happened with your father and the Clays was a very long time ago. The only one it still bothers seems to be you."

What happened with Max and Sarah was a long time ago, too, yet it still felt like yesterday. "Last I heard, she was studying finance. Didn't expect to find her here teaching third grade."

"I like her." Genna pointed the spoon. "Hand me the strainer."

He shook his head and drained the pasta himself. "You're supposed to be resting, Ma, not cooking up a storm like this."

"Consider it good planning. We'll have left-overs for a week."

He heard the crackle of his radio and went out to get it. He listened to the dispatch, answered, and stuck his head back in the kitchen. "Gotta go. You okay with Eli?"

She waved her wooden spoon. "Of course. Be careful, now."

He yelled up the stairs for Eli to mind his grandmother, and hustled out to the SUV.

The drive to the Double-C Ranch wasn't an unfamiliar one, though it had been a helluva long time since Max had made it. The ranch was the largest and most successful spread in the vicinity. It was owned by the Clays, though as far as Max knew, Sawyer—the sheriff—had never taken an active part in running it. That was the job of Matthew Clay.

Sarah's father.

He turned in through the gate and a short while later stopped in the curved drive behind Sawyer's cruiser. He could count on his hands the number of times he'd been to the Double-C. The last time, he'd been barely fifteen and his father had been caught red-handed stealing Double-C cattle.

It was still burned in his memory.

He climbed out of his truck, nodding at Sawyer, who was leaning against one of the stone columns on the front porch. "Matthew," he greeted the second man.

Sarah's father ambled down the steps, sticking his hand out. "Max. Good to see you again."

Max returned the greeting, looking past the man to his new boss. "What's up?"

"Thought it best to discuss things away from the station."

Max looked from Sawyer to his brother.

"He's aware of the situation," the older man said. "Let's walk."

"You're surprised," Matthew observed as they headed away from the house, cutting across the drive toward a sweeping, open area unoccupied by anything but a stand of mighty trees.

Max didn't like feeling out of control. Sawyer might be the sheriff, but the investigation was *Max's*. "It was my understanding that nobody but my superior and the sheriff knew what I was really doing here."

"Matt's noticed another discrepancy among his trucking records," Sawyer told him. "This time on a shipment of stock heading to Minnesota."

"How recent?"

"Couple weeks." Matt settled his cowboy hat deeper over his forehead. "When I talked to Sawyer about it, he admitted the other thing that's been going on." His face was grim. "Bad business. Kind of thing I don't want to see going on in Weaver."

"Drug trafficking shouldn't be going on *anywhere*," Max said flatly. For five years, he'd been serving on a special task force investigating distribution cells that were cropping up in small towns. The less traditional locations were highly difficult to pinpoint.

"You're right about that," Sawyer agreed. "Seems as if Weaver is just one more small town to become involved lately." He tilted his head back, studying the sun that hung low on the horizon. It wasn't quite evening yet, but the temperature was already dropping. "Much as I hate to admit it, we need help. That's why I didn't oppose your assignment here."

It wasn't exactly news to Max since he'd have done just about anything to get out of this particular assignment. But he was here now. He'd do his job.

He was a special agent with the DEA and it was one thing that he was usually pretty good at.

"I'm going to need the details about your discrepancies," he told Matthew.

The other man pulled an envelope out of his down vest and handed it over. "Copies and my notes."

Max didn't bother opening it now. He shoved it into his own pocket. "Anything else?"

"Matthew!"

All three men turned at the hail from the house.

"Supper's on!"

For a moment, Max thought the woman on the porch was Sarah. She bore an uncanny resemblance. But when she turned and went back inside, he didn't see that waist-length braid.

"Care to stay?" Matt offered. "My wife, Jaimie, is a pretty fine cook."

"Another reason why I'm out here," Sawyer admitted. "Bec—my wife—is in Boston on some medical symposium all this week. Been getting tired of my own cooking."

"Appreciate the offer," Max said. "But I need to get back to town."

"At least come in and say hello or Jaimie'll bug me from now until spring. Everyone in the county wants to greet the new deputy."

"Sure, until they start remembering the days when I lived here," Max countered. His father, Tony, might have been the criminal, but Max hadn't exactly been an altar boy. Getting friendly with the folks of Weaver was *not* in his plan. He was just there to do a job.

In that way, at least, he could make one thing right with the Clay family.

But after that, he and Eli would be gone.

Still, Max could read Sawyer's expression well enough. The steely-eyed sheriff expected Max to act neighborly.

"I'd be pleased to say hello," he said, feeling a tinge of what Eli must have been feeling when Max had lectured him on behaving well.

Matthew wasn't entirely fooled, as far as Max could tell, as they headed toward the house. They skirted the front porch entirely, going around, instead, to the rear of the house. They went in through the mudroom, and then into the cheery, bright kitchen.

"Don't get excited, Red, 'cause he's not

staying," Matthew said as they entered. "But this here's Sawyer's new right-hand man, Max Scalise."

Jaimie rubbed her hands down the front of the apron tied around her slender waist. "Of course. I remember you as a boy, Max." She took his hand in hers, shaking it warmly. "Genna talks of you often. She always has such fun sharing pictures from her trips out to see you and Eli. I know she must be so pleased that you're back in Weaver. How is her leg coming along?"

"More slowly than she'd like."

"Mom, I still can't find the lace—" Sarah entered the kitchen from the doorway opposite Max, and practically skidded to a halt. "Tablecloths," she finished. "What're *you* doing here?"

"Just picking up some paperwork from the sheriff," Max said into the silence that her abrupt question caused. "Nice to see you again, Miss Clay." He looked at Jaimie, who was eyeing him and her daughter with curiosity. "And it was nice to see you, too, ma'am."

"Give your mother my regards," Jaimie told him as he stepped toward the mudroom again.

"I'll do that. Sheriff. Matthew. See you later."

He was almost at his SUV when he heard footsteps on the gravel drive behind him.

"Max." Her voice was sharp.

The memory of that voice, husky with sleep, with passion, hovered in the back of his mind. He ought to have memories just as clear about Jennifer.

But he didn't.

He opened the SUV door and tossed the envelope from Matthew inside on the seat. "Don't worry, Sarah," he said, his voice flat. "I'm not *trying* to run into you every time we turn around."

She'd taken time only long enough to grab a sweater, and she held it wrapped tight around her shoulders. Tendrils of reddish-blond hair had worked loose from her braid and drifted against her neck. "Believe me," she said, her tone stiff, "I didn't once think that you *were*." She worked her hand out from beneath the sweater. She held an ivory envelope. "It's an invitation for your mother to my cousin's wedding."

He took the envelope, deliberately brushing her fingers with his.

The action was a double-edged sword, though.

She surrendered the envelope as if it burned her, and the jolt he'd felt left more than his fingertips feeling numb. "Ever heard of postage stamps?"

She didn't look amused. "Most of the invites are being hand-delivered because the wedding is so soon. Friday after Thanksgiving. We're all helping out with getting them delivered. Since your mom's in the same quilting group as Leandra's mother, they wanted her to have an invitation."

"Leandra?"

"My cousin. She's marrying Evan Taggart."

He remembered their names, of course. Taggart had grown up to become the local vet. Leandra was yet another one of the Clays and, he remembered, Sarah's favorite cousin. If he wasn't mistaken, he thought the vet had been on some television show Leandra had been involved with. More proof that Weaver wasn't quite so "small town" as it once was. "I'll make sure she gets it." He tapped the envelope against his palm. "Eli told me what he did today."

She pulled the dark blue sweater more tightly around her shoulders, and said nothing.

He exhaled, feeling impatience swell inside him. "Dammit, Sarah, at least *say* something."

Her ivory face could have been carved from ice. "Be careful driving back to Weaver. Road gets slick at night sometimes."

Then she turned on her heel, and for the third time that day, she walked away from him.

Chapter 3

Despite Sarah's hopes, days two, three and four of Eli Scalise were just as bad—or worse—than day one.

He didn't hit another student with a dodge ball, but he was still miles away from the model of behavior. A conversation with his previous school had told her that this was *not* the norm where Eli was concerned.

By Thursday, she knew she had to speak with Max about it. She hated the fact that several times throughout the day, she put off calling him. It showed her cowardice.

And since she was supposed to be *thoroughly* over the man, what did she have to be afraid of?

For another ten minutes or so, her students would still be in the cafeteria, practicing their part in the holiday program they'd present in less than a month. And Sarah had done enough dithering.

Nerves all nicely inflated, she snatched up the phone and dialed the sheriff's office. But Pamela Rasmussen, her uncle's newest dispatcher, told her that Max was out on a call.

"I can get a message to him if it's urgent. His son's okay, isn't he?"

Okay was a subjective term, Sarah thought. "It's not urgent. I'd appreciate you asking him to give me a call when he's free, though."

"Sure, Sarah. No prob. So, how are Leandra's wedding plans coming together?"

"Rapidly." Sarah was Leandra's maid of honor. "She's got so much going on with the start-up of Fresh Horizons that we're all doing as much as we can to take some of the wedding details off her shoulders." Fresh Horizons was Leandra's newly planned speech, physical and occupational therapy program. It would be located at her parents' horse farm, so they could utilize hippotherapy as a treatment strategy.

"Wouldn't mind taking the honeymoon off her shoulders," Pam said with a laugh. "Think Evan Taggart was one of the last hot bachelors around here. Everyone else seems too young for us. Or too old."

Sarah had an unwanted image of Max shoot into her brain. She knew he'd turned forty that year. His August birthday was just another one of those details about the man that she couldn't seem to get out of her head.

"Hadn't really thought about it," Sarah lied. "Thanks for leaving the message, Pam. Gotta run."

"You betcha."

She quickly hung up, then nearly jumped out of her skin when the phone rang right beneath her hand where it still rested on the receiver. She snatched it up. "Sarah Clay."

"Sounding sort of tense there, Sarah."

Her breath eked out. "Brody. What's wrong?"

"Nada. Kid's fine."

She looked toward the classroom door. She could hear footsteps outside in the corridor. "Then what are you calling me here for?" She made it a point not to blur the lines between her real life and her other job. It's the reason she'd been as successful at keeping that other duty under wraps as she had been.

Not even her family knew about it.

"Megan needs more schoolwork. She's already blown through the materials you left."

She wasn't surprised. Her few encounters

with Megan Paine had told her the girl was exceptionally bright. "Maybe you should just register her for classes." Her associate, Brody Paine, hadn't been entirely thrilled with the idea of homeschooling Megan. Presenting the child as his daughter while under his protection was one thing. Trying to keep the girl up on her schoolwork was another. Not even two months of it had made the man more comfortable with the situation.

"My daughter's not ready for that. She is still adjusting to her mother's death."

Sarah's nerves tightened a little. That was the cover, but she wasn't used to Brody using it when it was only the two of them. Which probably meant that Brody wasn't confident the school's line was secure.

The man was notoriously paranoid when it came to things like that.

"I see. You know best, I'm sure." Sarah wasn't so sure Brody was right on the school attendance, but she wasn't going to argue with him. He was a trained agent.

She was just a...go between.

It was a position she'd sort of fallen into.

The only good thing to have come out of her time in California. When Coleman Black had approached her, she'd been swayed by his passionate explanation of how a person like her was needed by the agency. She'd believed she'd been abandoned by Max and had just lost their child. She'd needed to *count.* To matter to this world in ways that had nothing to do with her family, with anyone else but her.

She and Brody had already discussed the matter at length. Who would expect Megan to be in Weaver, after all? That's what made Sarah's involvement these past years with the agency work so beautifully. Their charges—children who, for one reason or another needed more protection than could be provided through traditional avenues—could be hidden in plain sight. In Megan's case, her parents, Simon and Debra Devereaux—both mid-level politicians—had been brutally killed earlier that year. Hollins-Winword had become involved when other means to protect Megan—the only witness—had continually failed. The sight line of Weaver was pretty much off the radar unless you were a local rancher or worked for CeeVid, her uncle Tristan's gaming software design company.

Nine times now, she'd arranged the houses when Hollins-Winword contacted her.

Another agent—never the same one—came in with their assignment for a while, and then moved on when it was time. She never knew where the children went, only that they'd been found a permanent safe haven.

This time, the agent was Brody Paine. And it was his opinion that ruled, whether she considered him paranoid or not.

The footsteps outside in the hall sounded louder. "I'll pull some more work together for her. Want me to drive it out to you?" The safe house where Brody was staying with Megan was located about fifteen miles out of town. Located midway between nothing and more nothing.

"I'll pick it up sometime tomorrow."

She frowned a little, not liking the alarm that was forming inside her. "Brody—"

"Appreciate your help, Sarah. You're a good teacher." He severed the connection.

She slowly replaced the receiver. When she lifted her gaze to the doorway, though, Max Scalise stood there. The sight so surprised her that she actually gasped.

"Didn't mean to startle you."

Denying she had been would be foolish. She drew her hand back from the telephone and eyed him. "What are you doing here?"

His eyebrows rose a little. He wore the typical uniform of brown jacket and pants, his radio and badge hanging off his heavy belt that could also sport a weapon and a half-dozen other items, but currently didn't.

She realized her gaze had focused on his lean hips though, and looked back at his face. "You left *me* a message, remember?"

"Barely five minutes ago. I didn't expect you to show up here."

He closed the remaining distance between them and picked up the gleaming porcelain apple that she'd been given by a student at the end of last year. "What'd you want to see me about?"

She hadn't wanted to *see* him at all. "Eli cheated on his math test today."

His gaze sharpened on her face. "Eli doesn't cheat."

She pushed back from her chair and stood. Sitting there while he towered over her desk just put her at too much of a disadvantage. "Well, he did today. And he did yesterday. During the spelling test. He also tried to turn in another student's homework as his own."

A muscle flexed in his jaw, making the angular line even more noticeable. It was only one in the afternoon, yet he already had a blur of a five o'clock shadow. "He doesn't *need* to cheat," he said flatly.

According to her conversation with Eli's last school, that had been the story, too. Eli's grades hadn't been as high as they could be, but they'd been solid. "Maybe not, but that doesn't mean he didn't do it." She pulled out a slightly wrinkled piece of notebook paper and pointed at the corner where pencil marks had clearly been erased and overwritten with Eli's name.

"Any kid could have done that."

She exhaled and reminded herself that Max wasn't the first parent who didn't want to acknowledge some imperfection about their child. "Any kid didn't. Eli did."

He tossed the paper back on the desk. "Look, I know his first day here wasn't the best. But he's promised me that every day since he's been on his best behavior."

"And you believe him, unquestioningly?"

"He's my son."

She pressed her lips together for a moment. How well she knew that. "Yes, and it doesn't change the facts," she finally said, and hated that the words sounded husky. She cleared her throat. "Why don't we three meet together, later. After school. And we can talk about it then."

"I don't have time after school." He replaced the apple on the desk. "Maybe Eli would be better off with a different teacher."

Her fingers curled. "I'm the *only* third grade teacher here."

For the first time, he showed some sign of frustration. He pushed his long fingers through his short hair, leaving the black-brown strands rumpled. "Damn small town," he muttered.

Defensiveness swelled inside her. "You're the one who came back here, Max. Lord only knows why, after all this time." She felt the warmth in her cheeks and knew they probably looked red.

"I came for my mother's sake."

The dam of discretion she ordinarily possessed had sprung a leak, though. "How admirable of you. It's been once in…how long? Twenty years?" The last time he'd been in Weaver, she'd been all of six years old.

His lips tightened. "Twenty-two years, actually."

"Like I said." Her lips twisted. "Admirable."

"I'm not here to argue with you, Sarah. What happened in California between you and me was a long time ago."

Seven years. Four months. A handful of days. "If you think I'm holding the fact that you dumped me against your son, you're *way* off the mark."

"I didn't dump you."

She gave a short, humorless laugh. "That's exactly what you did. But it doesn't matter anymore. I never even think about it." *Liar, liar, pants on fire.*

"Then why the hell are you so angry?"

Her lips parted, but no answer came. She'd gotten over angry a very, very long time ago. But the hurt?

That was a much harder row to hoe. Chock-full of boulders and stone-hard dirt.

"Maybe I just don't understand why my uncle thought you'd be a good choice for deputy," she finally said.

His well-shaped lips thinned. "I am not my father."

"No, he just rustled Double-C cattle. You rustled—" She broke off, her face flushing again.

"Rustled what?" He planted his hands on the desk that stood between them and leaned over it. "You?"

She would have backed up if there hadn't been a wall right behind her. "There's not anything in Weaver that'll hold your interest for long. I think you'll get bored stiff catching the occasional speeder and settling disputes between Norma Cleaver and her neighbor over her dog barking at night, and you'll take off again, leaving my uncle to find yet *another* deputy."

"I think your uncle is capable of deciding whether or not that's a problem for him."

"I just don't like knowing my family is going to be disappointed by you."

He stifled an oath. "Jesus, Sarah. We saw each other for less than a month. Does it occur to you that you might be overreacting?"

Anger wasn't beyond her, after all. It curled low and deep inside her like a hot ember.

Mirroring his position, she pressed her hands against the edge of the desk and leaned forward. Close enough to see the individual lashes tangling around his green-brown eyes. To see that the faint crow's-feet beside those eyes had deepened and that an errant strand of silver threaded through his thick, lustrous hair, right above his left temple. "Dumping me was one thing. Lying to me was another."

"What, exactly, did I lie about?" he asked, his expression suddenly unreadable.

She could hear the roar of kids coming down the hall. Chorus practice was definitely over. "I'm not interested in giving you a list, Max. What would be the point? You know your own lies better than anyone." She pushed the homework page that Eli had swiped at him. "Talk to your *son,*" she said evenly, "about his behavior in school. We need to get this straightened out for his sake."

"Eli never had trouble in a class until now."

Meaning this was her fault?

She didn't reply. If she did, she'd lose her temper for certain.

Chrissy Tanner was the first student to round the classroom door, closely followed by several more, and Sarah was heartily glad to see them.

When Eli skidded around the corner, his eyeballs about bulged out of his head at the sight of his father standing there. He gave Sarah a furtive look as he gave his father a "yo" in greeting and headed to his lone table.

Max looked back at Sarah. The radio at his hip was crackling and he reached for it, automatically turning down the volume. "We'll finish this later."

It sounded more like a threat than a promise of parental concern.

And the problem was, Sarah didn't know *what* they were to finish discussing. The problems with Eli, or the past.

Once Max departed though, Sarah enjoyed one benefit from his unexpected appearance in her classroom. Eli didn't do one thing to earn a second glance from her for the remainder of the afternoon. He even offered to help clean up the counters after their science experiment.

She handed him the sponge. "Don't make me regret this," she murmured.

He gave her an angelic smile that she wanted to trust.

And aside from flicking water at Chrissy when she began telling him that he was sponging *all wrong*, he behaved.

In the end, as she was driving out to her aunt Emily's place later that evening, she decided to look on the afternoon as a success.

By the time she arrived at the horse farm that bordered a portion of the Double-C, Sarah was more than ready to put thoughts of both the Scalise men out of her head. And the evening of wedding planning with Leandra would surely provide enough distraction to do just that.

She didn't bother knocking on the door at the Clay Farm house. She'd grown up running in and out of Leandra's house just as comfortably as Lee had run in and out of the big house at the Double-C. The kitchen was empty and she headed through to the soaring great room. There, she hit pay dirt.

Leandra was standing on a chair, long folds of delicate fabric flowing around her legs while her fiancé's mother, Jolie Taggart, crouched around the hem, studying it closely.

"Looks serious," Sarah said.

Leandra shot her a harried look. "I never should have thought it was a good idea to wear a wedding gown. Who am I kidding? I've already done the whole white wedding thing. People are going to think we're ridiculous."

"The only thing people are going to think is that they wish they were as lucky as you, getting married to the person you love."

Leandra had come back to Weaver only a few months ago to shoot a television show featuring their old friend, Evan Taggart, who was the local veterinarian. The show had been a success, but even more successful was the love they'd managed to find along the way.

"And besides, you're not wearing white," Sarah pointed out. "You're wearing yellow."

"Hint of Buttercup," Emily Clay corrected blithely. She sat to one side with Sarah's mother, Jaimie, watching the fitting. "And if you'd wanted to elope with Evan, you've had ample time to do so."

"Well, thanks for the sympathy, Mom." But Leandra was smiling faintly, even though she was dragging her fingers through her short, wispy hair. She turned her gaze on Sarah.

"I'm telling you. When you get married, just pick the shortest route between you and the preacher, and forget all this folderol."

"I'd need a date with a man first before I could entertain such lofty notions as marriage." Sarah dropped the box of soft gold bows that she'd picked up in town on the floor beside her mother and aunt. "We just need to attach the flower sprays with hot glue. Glue guns are in the box, too," she told them, then looked back at Leandra. "And you're just stressing because you're trying to do too many things at once. Put together a wedding in about a month's time and take care of all the details for Fresh Horizons."

"Speaking of which—" Leandra jumped on the topic "—I wondered if you'd mind helping me look through the resumes of all the therapists that I've received."

Sarah immediately started to nod, only to stop and eye her cousin suspiciously. "How many are there?"

Leandra lifted her shoulders, looking innocent.

Sarah was reminded of Eli's habit of making that sort of shrug, accompanied by that sort of look. Usually, when she'd pretty much caught him red-handed at something. "That many, huh?"

"Yeah. Nice problem to have, though, right? We figured it would be hard to find a therapist willing to come to Weaver to staff the program. Even though our focus will be the use of hippotherapy—I mean this *is* a horse farm, and we've got the best pick of animals to train for it—there could well be situations when hippotherapy isn't the strategy that the therapist will want to use." Animation lit her cousin's features as she lifted her arms to her side. "Anyway, we've got a *huge* stack of resumes to go through. It's great."

"Keep still, honey," Jolie said around a mouthful of stickpins.

Leandra lowered her arms. "Sorry."

"Good thing your future mother-in-law is better with a needle than I am," Emily observed, grinning. She, like Jaimie, held a margarita glass in her hand.

Jolie carefully placed another pin. "Never fixed a wedding gown that was six inches too long before, though." She looked up at Leandra, smiling. "And stressful or not, my son will fall in love with you all over again when he sees you in this."

Sarah sank down in an oversized leather chair and stretched her legs out in front of her. "The sooner you settle on a therapist, the sooner we can get the brochures out to the schools and agencies in the area. I was at a meeting recently and three other teachers had families that they *know* will be interested in your program." She glanced around and saw no evidence of a child around. "Where's Hannah, anyway?" Hannah was Evan's niece, for whom he had guardianship, and was Leandra's inspiration for realizing that Weaver and the area surrounding it needed more specialized services available for children with developmental and physical disabilities. She'd felt so strongly about it that she'd even given up her hard-won promotion on the television series.

"With Evan. They went to Braden to see her grandparents for a few hours."

"I'm glad Sharon stopped fighting Evan on Hannah's guardianship." Jolie stuck her unused pins into a red pincushion and sat back to study her efforts with Leandra's hem. "Poor woman has lost her daughter—poor Darian, too—but neither one of them are up to the task of dealing with Hannah's autism."

Sarah was watching Leandra's face. She'd lost a daughter, too, only Emi had been a toddler. Sharon and Darian's daughter, Katy, had been serving in the military and up until recently, they'd been caring for Katy's four-year-old daughter, Hannah. "How's Hannah adjusted to you moving to Evan's place?" She was concerned for the little girl, but she was also concerned for her cousin, who'd blamed herself for the loss of Emi.

Leandra's gaze, when it met Sarah's, told her she understood exactly what Sarah meant. "We're all adjusting just fine." Her lips curved. "And Evan's learning what it's like to be outnumbered by females under his own roof."

"Don't think he's suffering too badly," Jolie observed, looking amused. "You can take off the dress, honey, but watch the pins."

Leandra gingerly stepped off the chair, holding the long folds up and baring the thick red-and-black argyle socks she was wearing.

"Nice fashion touch there."

Leandra rolled her eyes. "Give me a break. This is the first winter I've spent in Wyoming in a long time. It's *cold!*"

The rest of them just laughed.

"Come help me get out of this thing," Leandra bid as she passed Sarah. Jolie had pushed herself off the floor and was helping herself to the pitcher of margaritas that Emily and Jaimie were already sampling. Sarah rose and followed her cousin out of the great room and up the stairs to Leandra's childhood bedroom. Little had changed there since they'd been teenagers. Except the posters of Leandra's favorite rock star were gone.

"So—" Leandra said, the moment they closed the door "—how's it going with Eli? More to the point, how is it going with Max?"

"There's *nothing* going with Max." Sarah began unfastening the long, *long* line of pearl-like buttons stretching from Leandra's nape to below her waist. "I thought these things were just for looks," she said. "You know, to hide a sensible zipper or something that won't take a week to unfasten."

"But you've seen him since Eli's first day at school, right?"

Her cousin knew that she'd run into Max at her folks' place, because Sarah had told her. And her cousin also knew why it mattered, because Leandra was the only one Sarah had ever told about her ill-fated affair with the man. She was the only one who'd known about Sarah's pregnancy.

About the miscarriage that followed.

"He came by the school today," she admitted. "To discuss Eli."

"And?"

"And nothing." She slipped a few more buttons free. "I think you can step out of the dress now."

Her cousin did a little shimmy and pushed

the fabric down over her slender hips. Sarah took the dress and held it up while Leandra pulled on a dark brown velvety sweat suit. "This dress is so beautiful," she murmured.

Leandra took the dress and carefully laid it aside on the foot of the bed. Then she took Sarah's hands in hers. "*Talk* to me."

"There's nothing to talk about. Truly." She squeezed her cousin's fingers, then headed for the door. "Come on. Margaritas and glue guns are waiting."

"You know, you were the one who kept telling me I needed to talk about Emi."

"You did need to talk about her. But there's a world of difference between that and what happened between Max and me."

"You were in love with the man."

Sarah wrapped her fingers around the doorknob. "I *thought* I was," she corrected. "A big difference."

Leandra just looked concerned. She picked up her wedding gown. "Is it?"

"Look, don't worry about me. I'm a big girl. Eli is the only challenge I have where the Scalise family is concerned."

Leandra followed her into the hallway and toward the stairs. Her gown rustled softly as they walked. "Then you won't be bothered at all by knowing that your mom has invited

Genna Scalise and Max and Eli over for Thanksgiving dinner next Thursday."

Sarah stopped dead at the head of the stairs. "What? How do you know that?"

"Before you got here, your mom and mine and Jolie were all talking about Thanksgiving dinner. The only place with a large enough dining room to seat *everyone* and still be inside, is at the big house."

"Which has what to do with Max?"

Leandra looked knowing. "Sounding a little perturbed considering his presence isn't bugging the life out of you."

"Leandra—"

Her cousin looked slightly repentant. "Sawyer really likes Max, Sarah."

"I assumed he must or he wouldn't have hired him." She didn't like the increasingly dry feeling in her mouth.

"Did you know that Sawyer is thinking about retiring? He and Dad were talking about it the other day."

For as long as Sarah could remember, her uncle had been sheriff of Weaver. He was as popular as he was effective. "No, but it doesn't seem unreasonable, given how long he's served. But what does that have— Oh, no. *No*." She shook her head. "If Sawyer thinks Max might be a good replacement, he's way off base."

They heard a low, melodious chime and Leandra looked down the staircase. The foyer below was empty, but they could hear peals of female laughter coming from the great room, and footsteps heading toward the front door. "You want to go to Sawyer and tell him just why you feel that way?" She lifted her brows, waiting for a moment. "I didn't think so."

"And since Sawyer thinks he can groom Max to be his replacement, he invited them all for Thanksgiving dinner. Just one big happy—" Sarah's throat tightened "—family."

"That's what it looks like to me." Voices from the foyer floated up to them. "I figured you might want a heads-up." Leandra started down the steps when people came into view, only to stop short. "Evan!" She suddenly turned to Sarah and thrust the gown into her arms. "Bad luck. Bad luck. We don't need any bad luck." Then she hurried down the staircase to hug her fiancé.

Sarah would have laughed at the sudden comedy of the moment if she hadn't also noticed the other man who'd entered behind Evan.

Max.

Dealing with him because of Eli was difficult enough.

So why did he have to keep popping up everywhere *else* she turned, too?

And why, if she'd put him in the past the way she kept telling herself, did that fact bother her quite so much?

Chapter 4

From his position at the base of the wide, curving staircase, Max could see the color drain right out of Sarah's face when she looked down and saw him.

Once again, when it came to Sarah, his timing couldn't have been worse.

She stood there, clutching a hank of buttery colored fabric that streamed down around her legs. Given the other woman's panicked reaction, he supposed it must be a wedding dress. He could remember Jennifer having a similar reaction when E.J. had seen the wedding dress she was to have worn for *their* wedding.

The bad luck that had struck there, though, hadn't been caused at all by Jennifer.

That had been Max's doing.

He looked at the petite blonde who was eyeing him speculatively. She looked vaguely familiar, which meant he'd either known her as a girl, or she was kin to the rest of the Clays. Probably both.

Emily Clay was smiling at him. "Max, you might not remember my daughter, Leandra. Honey, this is Max Scalise." Her brown gaze turned back to him. "We've been talking about you this evening, I'm afraid. So if your ears have been ringing, blame us."

Max stuck out his hand toward Leandra. The favorite cousin. Did she know about his past with Sarah? "Nice to see you again." When he'd left Weaver, he'd been eighteen and she'd have been just as young a girl as Sarah had been. But he remembered Sarah talking about her cousin when they'd known each other in California.

Known.

What a pitiful word to describe those few brief, memorable weeks.

Leandra shook his hand, but it was brief. She didn't return his greeting, though she managed a cordial enough smile.

Oh yeah, he thought silently. Favorite cousin knew chapter and verse just what had occurred between Sarah and him.

"We drove up at the same time," Evan said, breaking the infinitesimal lull that marked Leandra's silence.

The small, dark-haired girl who'd insisted on ringing the doorbell stood half-hiding behind Evan's legs, not looking at Max at all. Hannah, the other man had introduced while they'd been out on the porch.

Cute kid. Definitely shy. Looked a lot like her uncle.

Max had already checked out Evan Taggart, though the sheriff had discounted him as being involved with the trafficking. But Max liked to form his own opinions. The guy did seem like a straight shooter, though. Max even knew about Taggart's recently awarded guardianship of his niece.

"I'm here to see Jefferson." Max focused on Emily.

"Right. He mentioned that you'd phoned." She showed no hesitation in the way her daughter had, but tucked her hand under his arm and drew him farther into the house. "He's downstairs, I think. Took shelter there in the face of too much wedding talk."

Max couldn't help himself.

He glanced up toward Sarah, still standing there like a statue above them all, her reddish hair a gilded crown that flowed down past her shoulders.

When his gaze met hers, though, she turned on her heel and retreated up the two steps she'd managed to descend. A moment later, he heard a door close.

Her walking away from him was becoming a seriously irritating habit.

Emily ushered him down to the basement that really wasn't like any basement that Max had ever experienced. There was no sight of a washer and dryer, no furnace, no jumble of old bicycles and discarded furniture. Instead, there was the crackle of a fire burning in a stone fireplace, oversized leather couches and chairs scattered around it, and a big-screen television that took up a good portion of one wall.

"Max." Jefferson Clay greeted him with a brief nod. Not an unfriendly one, though. Just to the point, the way Max remembered. "Come on in. I've pulled the records you asked me to."

"I know you won't mind, so I'll excuse myself," Emily said. "Margaritas are calling." She sent Max a friendly smile and headed back toward the stairs. "We have plenty to share once you're finished here."

Jefferson's gaze followed his wife's departure for a moment before he returned his attention to Max. He led the way into another room—clearly an office, though in Max's opinion, the furnishings were a helluva lot nicer than what filled the sheriff's office. Those leaned more toward scarred metal desks and chairs right out of the 60s. Functional was the kindest description there.

The other man lifted a manila folder that contained at least a half-inch of papers off the massive teak desk. "Fortunately, my wife is the accountant in the family," Jefferson said. "Because personally, I hate paperwork. All the trucking records are here. What are you looking for particularly?"

"A common thread." Max took the folder. In the past few days, he'd talked with nearly all of Sawyer's brothers about the investigation.

"Good luck finding it," Jefferson said. "I've been through it all and didn't see anything amiss. But maybe fresh eyes are what's needed."

Max grimaced wryly. "Been a long time since I've considered much of anything about myself to be particularly fresh."

Jefferson's lip quirked. "I hear you there. But I'll still suggest you wait another passel of years before you say that. How's Genna healing up?"

"Too slowly to suit her." He tapped the folder. "Appreciate the hard copies." Max hadn't wanted faxes going in or out of the station house. He wasn't going to do anything to raise questions about what he was doing that he didn't want raised. "I'll make sure you get them back."

"Shred 'em," Jefferson said. "I've got the originals." He leaned back against the desk, crossing one boot over the other at the ankles. He looked casual. Interested. Friendly.

Like most of the Clays had.

Except Sarah.

He hadn't really expected warmth from any of the Clays after what his father had done. He wouldn't have blamed them if they'd wanted nothing to do with Tony Scalise's son. But Sarah—*that* had nothing to do with Tony and everything to do with Max.

"You're settling in again all right here?" Jefferson asked.

The question came out of nowhere. As unexpectedly as Sawyer's insistence that Max and his family join the Clays for Thanksgiving. If it hadn't been for Genna and Eli, Max would have happily declined. But his mother and son deserved *some* sort of Thanksgiving celebration. "Except for freezing my ass off," Max answered smoothly. He wasn't particularly joking.

Jefferson's lips quirked again with faint amusement. But it didn't really extend to his eyes. "Most folks figure coming home is always an easy thing to do."

Another unexpected observation. Only Max knew that in his day, Jefferson had spent a fair period of time away from Weaver, himself. "I'm not 'home' in that sense," Max corrected easily. "This is just an assignment."

The older man eyed Max for a silent moment. Then he nodded. Whether in agreement or acceptance or amusement, Max couldn't tell.

Not that it mattered, anyway.

"Appreciate this." He tapped the folder. "I'll let you get back to enjoying your evening now."

Jefferson didn't argue and they headed back upstairs. Emily spotted them before Max could make for the door, though. "You have to come in and have something to drink."

"Afraid margaritas are not on the menu for me, ma'am. I'm on duty." Not technically, but he didn't figure anyone there would argue the point.

Particularly Sarah, who was sitting on

the floor, surrounded by a dozen intricately shaped bows. She had warily tracked him from the moment he entered the room.

"We've got coffee, too," Emily assured. "Come on. I can't send you back out in this temperature without putting something warm inside you. Did you know it's ten degrees colder than it normally is this time of year?"

Despite himself, Max smiled. The woman was hospitality in motion.

From her niece, Sarah, though, he could practically feel the waves of animosity directed toward him.

And since he'd always been an ornery cuss, he changed his mind about leaving. "Feel's more like twenty degrees," he told Emily. "And coffee would be welcome. Thank you."

At his hip, his radio crackled with a call being sent to one of the other deputies on duty. He turned down the volume a little more.

There were plenty of places to sit in the great room. It probably wasn't the smartest thing he'd ever done in his life, but he took the seat closest to where Sarah was sitting on the rug.

Her long jeans-clad legs were folded cross-legged, and she had her head bent over one of the bows and some flowery-looking thing that reminded him a little of the weeds that grew wild in the culverts.

Against the white sweater she wore, her shining hair looked more red than blond. It was nearly as long as it had been seven years ago.

There was no way she could be unaware of him in the seat barely two feet away from her knee, but she didn't look up at him.

"Here you go, Max." Emily handed him a thick white mug full of steaming brew. "Sugar? Cream?"

"Black's fine, thanks."

She gave him another smile.

His mother had always claimed that the Clay family was fair and generous. Before he'd left Weaver, he'd never allowed himself to acknowledge whether or not that was true.

"Excuse me." Sarah reached past him for the box sitting beside his chair. She still didn't look at him, though, as she withdrew another bow.

Not the smartest thing he'd ever done, he thought again. Something that had always been a problem where Sarah was concerned.

"What are you doing?"

Her gaze flicked to the other occupants of the room. Leandra sat with her own collection of bows. Beside her, Hannah was running a toy car up and down her leg. Evan and Jefferson were talking about some horse and the three older women were chattering away a mile a minute, probably running on margarita fuel.

"More to the point—" her voice was low as she looked back at the items in her lap "—what are *you* doing?"

"Drinking coffee." He lifted the mug. "You're probably familiar with the act, despite that." He nodded toward the half-full margarita glass by her side.

"Where's Eli?"

"At home. With his grandmother. That a problem for you?"

The fine line of her jaw flexed slightly. She glanced around again. "Not as long as he's doing his *own* homework." Her voice was dulcet. "And you know good and well I'm not talking about coffee." She picked up the small glue gun beside her and dabbed melted glue on the bow, then stuck the flowery piece in it and set it aside with the growing stack of glued-up bows.

He sat forward, his arms resting on his thighs. This close to her, he could smell the fragrance of that long, beautiful hair.

It used to smell like lemons.

Now, he couldn't put his finger on the scent, but it was soft, womanly and seductive.

Damned heady, too.

He wrapped his fingers around the mug. He kept his voice low. For her ears only. "You hate all your old lovers with this much passion, Sarah?" He had no business wondering how many there might have been. No business caring.

He wondered anyway.

Cared anyway.

She snatched up another bow. "Only the ones who lie as easily as they breathe."

"I didn't lie to you."

She snorted softly and squirted glue out on the bow. Slapped a flower on it, then cursed softly, lifting her finger to her lips to blow on it.

"Did you burn yourself?"

"Seems to be my problem when you're in the vicinity." Her cheeks colored and she focused on her finger, peeling off the strings of glue that clung to it.

"You knew I tried to stay away from you." God, he'd tried. But she'd been the only fresh, unsullied person in his life back then. Everything else had been going to hell, but Sarah had been… Sarah.

He could still remember the day he'd

walked into Frowley-Hughes and came face-to-face with a woman who'd made him nearly forget his own name. Then when he'd learned *hers*—that she was one of those little Clay kids from back home, all grown up—he'd hung around to catch her after work. Just to make sure she didn't blow his cover.

And he'd been too damn weak to resist basking in her.

For just a while. Until the responsibilities in his life couldn't be ignored, couldn't be put off any longer.

But after he'd ended it, he'd never forgotten her.

Nor forgiven himself.

She'd gone still. "You should have tried harder," she finally said, her voice nearly inaudible. Then she yanked on the electric cord plugging the glue gun into an outlet behind his chair and rose, gathering up her materials. "Leandra, I've gotta run. I'll take these home and finish them up later."

"But—" Leandra started to rise, but Sarah was already hustling out of the room, a box of bows bumping against her slender hip.

Max watched her go. He set his unfinished coffee on the side table next to her unfinished margarita and quickly bid his own goodbyes. He didn't even care if the rest thought his departure after Sarah's had anything to do with her.

She wasn't twenty-one anymore, after all.

But by the time he made it out to his SUV, Sarah was already gone.

He yanked open the door, cursing under his breath. He tossed the manila folder inside and climbed behind the wheel. Going after her would be *beyond* stupid.

She'd made her feelings more than plain. She had no affection for him lingering inside her. No soft and sweet memories of the time they'd spent together when he'd been a narcotics detective and she'd been a finance intern.

When he'd learned that he could be just as content sitting beside her on a beach towel as he could be burying himself inside her sweet warmth.

She'd been left with something completely opposite. So much so that she couldn't even seem to separate her feelings about Max from Eli.

The gravel crunched beneath his wheels as he headed away from Emily and Jefferson's place. A few snowflakes hit his windshield.

Going after her would be pointless.

Out of habit, he called in his location. He would be the last one called if something came up. The sheriff didn't want Max tied up with dozens of mundane calls when he had higher priorities. But he also had to respond to enough calls to keep up appearances.

At the gate, he turned on the highway heading toward Weaver. He flipped the heater up another notch.

The highway was empty, the pavement stretching out in front of his vehicle in a dark, snaking path, illuminated by nothing except his headlights where snowflakes danced in the beams. There were no city lights. No high-rises. No billboards.

Except for the unexpected sprawl of growth Weaver had experienced, nothing about the place had really changed since Max left it all those years ago.

He saw the small blue sedan before long. Driving well within the speed limit. Obeying all the rules of the road.

She'd always been a little rule-follower.

Conscientious and conservative and cool, despite the red in her hair.

His foot gained some weight and the SUV inexorably began closing the distance between them. He turned on his beacon and pulled up behind the sedan when she slowed and veered off to the side of the road.

Once parked, she didn't wait inside her

car, though, the way she should have. She shoved open the door, stepped out onto the soft shoulder and strode toward him, meeting him halfway.

"Are you out of your mind?" She shocked the hell out of him when she pushed her hands against his chest and shoved him. "You nearly scared the life out of me!"

He steadied himself easily enough. "Assaulting an officer, Miz Clay?" He peered into her face, brilliantly illuminated by his strobes.

Oh, yeah. He was a stupid damn fool is what he was.

"Give me a break." She glared at him.

"Have you been drinking, ma'am?"

She crossed her arms tightly over her chest, which only drew his attention to the fact that she hadn't pulled on her coat, but stood there in the light snowfall wearing narrow jeans and that white cable-knit sweater. "You're abusing your authority here, Max. Think that's wise for the future sheriff of Weaver?"

He jerked his head back. "What the hell are you talking about?"

She sniffed. "As if you didn't know. So—" she tossed her arms out dramatically "—am I being stopped for drinking half a margarita, the audacity of suggesting your son cheated today, or am I being stopped for my monumentally bad judgment to have fallen for your line seven years ago?"

"I never gave you a *line.*" His voice was tight. "And I'm sorry that you were hurt when I broke it off. You knew it would happen though, because I told you it couldn't last. I told you and you insisted that it didn't matter, that the only thing that mattered was the here and now. And dammit to hell, I *knew* better than to believe you really felt that way. You were hardly more than a kid." Annoyed that he'd stopped her, annoyed that he was there in Wyoming in the first place, annoyed that he still wanted the woman, he turned away from her.

It was either that or kiss her.

He was an idiot, but he wasn't that much of one.

"I wasn't a kid."

"Fine." He looked back at her. "You weren't. You were a legal adult. Yet in comparison to me, you were a babe in the woods. And the hell of it is, if *anyone* fell for someone's line, it was probably me. Because I fooled myself into thinking that you *weren't* going to get burned in the end."

She was still staring at him as if he possessed three heads. "It wasn't a line, you stupid jerk. It was the way I felt. *I* didn't lie to you!"

"Meaning that I did?" Showing none of the control he was ordinarily famous for, he grabbed her shoulders, ignoring the squeaky gasp she made, and hauled her two inches from his nose. "Stop tossing out accusations like that. What exactly did I lie about, Sarah? *What?*"

She was trembling.

From cold or from his appalling behavior, he didn't know.

He only knew that, once again, every action he took when it came to Sarah was the wrong one.

He exhaled roughly. Deliberately set her back on her heels and started to let her go.

"You didn't tell me about Eli. And you didn't tell me that barely two weeks after you *broke it off* with me, you were marrying his *mother*."

He hadn't fooled himself into believing that Sarah didn't know he'd been married, but he damn sure didn't expect her to know it had happened right after he'd stopped seeing her. "Dammit, Sarah, my marriage to Jen was—"

"Don't!" Her voice rose. "Just don't. I might have been foolish enough to fall into your bed, Max, but do you honestly think I'd have done that if you'd told me you were engaged to be married? That you were already involved with someone else? That you had a child with her?" Her voice broke over the last and she shrugged out of his hold.

"I saw you, you know. On your wedding day. I stood by a bush and watched you exchange vows with her, while you held your son against your shoulder. There wasn't a single thing seven years ago that you *didn't* lie about, Max. From start, when you pretended to be a client at Frowley-Hughes, to finish."

She knew good and well that he'd been conducting an investigation at Frowley. He'd only told her to keep from blowing his cover. They might not have had much to do with one another in Weaver before he'd left, given their age differences, but she damn sure knew who he was.

His father had been convicted of rustling cattle from her father's ranch, for God's sake.

"I was on an assignment."

"And you were worried I might spill the beans," she snapped back. "You could have just asked me to keep quiet. You didn't have to pretend you—" She caught her hair in one hand, keeping it from blowing across her face. The snowfall was beginning to gain momentum. "Forget it. Just forget it. It's old news anyway. Water under the bridge." She reached for her car door. "Now, *Deputy*, do you mind if I get back in my car and drive away? Or are you going to haul me in on some trumped-up excuse?"

Pretend what? That he'd loved her? "I didn't pretend that I loved you." His voice was quiet, but it still carried to her. "And I wasn't engaged to Jennifer when I was with you. When I was with you, I was *only* with you. I can explain it all."

Her shoulders stiffened. The fingers clutching her thick, wind-tossed hair, tightened. "Save it. I don't even care anymore."

"Is that so? *Now* who is lying?"

She didn't answer. And after a silent moment that stretched on too long, she yanked open her car door and climbed inside.

A moment later, she set the car in gear, and pulled off the shoulder, back onto the empty, snow-dusted highway.

Max brushed a snowflake off his face, watching the red taillights until he could no longer see them. Then he climbed back in the SUV.

He'd known coming back to Weaver would be a mistake.

He just hadn't realized that mistake would include the ones that he'd already made—and continued to make—with Sarah Clay.

Chapter 5

By Saturday morning, the stack of bows in Sarah's living room were finished. She'd also finished tying pretty ribbons around a couple hundred little net packets of birdseed, and had addressed nearly that many place cards with gold calligraphy. She'd even printed up the signs to be used for the upcoming fund-raiser boutique at her school that she was in charge of, and made lists of all the merchants she needed to contact for donations.

She'd done all that, taught school and even had time to spring clean her house—even though spring seemed eons away given the snow that had been falling since the evening she'd spent at Clay Farm. She'd done her laundry. She'd done her manicure. Her pedicure. She'd written up her lesson plans from now until the end of the school year.

What she hadn't done was sleep.

Not Thursday night.

Not Friday night.

How could she when every time she closed her eyes, every time she felt herself falling asleep, she couldn't keep her guard up against thoughts of Max?

Now, it was Saturday morning.

Snow was mounded up against her front door and drifts were piled in her driveway. The few cars that had been parked on the street were unrecognizable because of the snow covering the tops of them.

There was not one single thing Sarah could do inside her house to keep herself busy. Not unless she started stripping wallpaper from her kitchen walls.

She recognized that giving Max that much power over her was really beyond pathetic, and she knew it was time to get away from the house. She bundled up in coat and scarf, went out the back door that was fortunately not blocked by a snow drift, and slowly made her way down the street.

It was still early. Only a few people were starting to emerge from their warm cocoons with snow shovels or snowblowers in hand. The sky was an unearthly white-blue, perfectly devoid of clouds. The air, so cold it burned if she inhaled too deeply. Even though it wasn't a far walk to Ruby's Café—just a few miles down to the end of her street and around the corner a ways—she was huffing by the time she made it there.

It was a relief to see a car parked outside on the street. She hadn't entirely been certain the place would be open, given the snow.

Inside, Evan Taggart's little sister, Tabby, was putting coffee in the filter and her smile was rueful as she greeted Sarah. "It may be just you and me here this morning," she said. "Justine's never late, but she is this morning." Justine Leoni was the granddaughter of Ruby Leoni, the café's founder, and now ran the place.

"Half the town is probably blocked in by snow." Sarah unwound the scarf around her head and hung it over the back of one of the stools at the counter. She dragged off her coat and shook out her hair, then slipped onto the stool. "How's school going?"

Tabby was a senior in high school. She was smart and bright and as shiny as a new tack. She made Sarah—short of sleep and feeling generally stressed out—feel older than the hills.

Tabby was nodding. Smiling. "Good. Glad we have a break for Thanksgiving next week, though."

"Been looking at colleges yet?"

"I want to study abroad. My parents—well, my mom mostly—is having a fit about it."

Sarah could well imagine. "My folks weren't thrilled when I went out to California, either." But they hadn't tried to stop her.

She almost wished that they had.

But it was pointless wishing over the past. She'd learned that a long time ago, when she hadn't even been left with the baby she'd realized too late that she'd desperately wanted.

"It's just because they'll miss you," Sarah told the girl. "They'll get used to the idea. Give them time. And it doesn't hurt to have some alternatives in your mind, as well. You might be the one to change your mind." Goodness knows she certainly had. She still couldn't fathom why she'd ever thought she'd be happy in finance when she was so satisfied now working with children.

"Oh, I know. I've already taken my entrance exams. I have applications in at several universities." The teenager flipped over a mug in front of Sarah. "Coffee will be a few minutes, yet. You want me to toss something on the grill for you?"

The idea of eating wasn't overly appealing. "Just some toast."

"Sure thing. Here." Tabby handed over the small remote control for the minuscule television that sat behind the counter. "If you want some noise. I'll be in the back for a few minutes." She popped some bread into the toaster and went through the swinging double doors that led to the kitchen.

Sarah wasn't opposed to sitting in the quiet café, listening to the sounds of Tabby getting the place ready for the day. But she hit the power button, anyway. The television came on. Morning news from the station in Cheyenne.

Above average snowfall all across the state.

She propped her chin on her hand and closed her eyes, letting the soft drone of the weather report flow over her. When she heard the toaster pop, she went around the counter and plopped the toast on a plate. Found a few pats of butter in the cooler and returned to her stool.

But once she'd buttered the toast, it held little interest. She took a few bites anyway. Going without any real sleep was one thing. Going without food for another meal was going to lead to her passing out.

The sound of the door opening behind her preceded a rush of cold air that invaded the comforting warmth of the diner. She looked over her shoulder and smiled when she saw her uncle. "Sawyer. You're out and about awfully early."

He yanked off his lined gloves as he made his way between the empty tables to the counter. He dropped a kiss on her cheek. "Could say the same about you, squirt." He took the stool beside her and began working out of his shearling coat. "It's barely daylight yet."

"Toast was calling me." She lifted one of the half-eaten slices and took another bite. "Is Rebecca still out of town?"

"Comes back tomorrow." He jerked his chin toward the swinging doors. "Justine back there?"

"Tabby."

He grunted a little. "Sent the snowplow out Justine's way. She'll be in soon enough, I 'spect. That coffee been on long?"

Sarah hid a smile and went around the counter again. She poured her uncle a mug of coffee, but handed him a saucer as well. Sure enough, he balanced the nearly flat saucer with the fingers of one hand and poured the steaming hot brew into it. She was still blowing on the coffee in her mug when he'd drunk down half of his, thanks to the way it cooled rapidly in the saucer.

"How's the new boy in your class doing? Eli?"

If it weren't for Sarah's history with Eli's father, she wouldn't have thought twice about Sawyer's interest. The man pretty much knew everything that went on in town. As a result, she forced herself to respond naturally.

"Settling in." A huge example of misinformation. Eli wasn't settling in well at all. Nor had he been in school the previous day. When she'd questioned the office about his absence, she'd learned only that his grandmother had called him in. "Hear anything from Ryan yet?"

Ryan was Sawyer and Rebecca's oldest. He was also the oldest of all of Sarah's cousins, and for the past few months, he'd been out of touch with the family.

Since Ryan served in the navy, it was a significant worry. Whatever assignment he'd been on was classified. They didn't even know what part of the world he was in.

Sawyer shook his graying head. "It's been five months now."

Sarah hid a sigh. She squeezed her uncle's hand. "He'll come home."

"Yeah." He lifted the saucer and refilled it.

His expression was grim and she knew that worry about Ryan was taking its toll.

She also knew that he'd think it unnatural for her not to ask about the newest member of *his* department. "What about Max Scalise? He settling in?"

Sawyer merely nodded. Which made Sarah wonder if his response was as truthful as hers had been about Eli.

"You gonna eat that toast, or look at it?" he asked.

She happily slid the plate toward him.

Then Tabby reappeared and Justine walked in with another rush of cold air. "Sarah. Sheriff," she greeted as she headed around the counter. "Thanks for the digging out this morning. Snow was halfway up my house." She poured herself some coffee and pressed open one of the swinging doors. "Breakfast's on me this morning, if you're taking."

"I am. How long before you've got some cinnamon rolls?"

The woman grinned. "Give me twenty."

"Ten," Tabby corrected. "I've already got 'em in the oven."

"Good girl," Sawyer said, feelingly.

"Your new deputy is on his way in, too," Justine said. "He was pulling into the parking lot right behind me. You still wanting hot rolls for the school's boutique, Sarah?"

Sarah had stiffened. "As many as you can bake up," she told Justine. She wasn't up to an encounter with Max just yet, particularly when she hadn't yet recovered from the last one. She dropped a few dollars on the counter for her toast and coffee, then reached for her scarf and flipped it around her neck.

"Leaving already?" Sawyer shot her a curious look.

"You know how it is with a wedding approaching. Maid of honor's work is never done." She gave him a quick hug and headed to the door, pulling on her coat as she went.

Max entered, just as she reached it, and she gave him a brusque nod. "Deputy. Hope Eli is all right." What she really wanted to ask was if he'd kept his son out of class because he really thought she was such a rotten teacher.

"Might be coming down with a cold," he said.

She fumbled with her coat buttons, very aware of their small audience. "If he's out more than a few days, I can send home some schoolwork so he doesn't fall behind." She finally fit the button in place, and flipped her hair out of her collar. "Otherwise, I guess I'll see y'all on Thanksgiving." She reached for the door, but he beat her to it, his hand brushing hers on the crash bar.

"Sarah." His voice was low. "Don't keep walking away from me."

"Have a nice day." She pushed through, anyway. The only reason her eyes were suddenly stinging, she assured herself, was because of the bitter cold.

A few cars were slowly driving down Main Street, where Ruby's was located, and she returned a wave or two as she hustled across the street once they'd passed. When she arrived at her little house across the street from the snowy park a short while later, she wasn't sure if she was surprised or not that Max hadn't followed her.

Not that she'd wanted him to.

Lord, no.

She went in through the back again, because—naturally—the snow blocking the front hadn't magically disappeared. She bypassed the neat piles of completed wedding projects sitting on every available surface in her kitchen, and went into her excruciatingly clean living room.

And then she just stood there, not knowing *what* to do.

Everywhere she turned these days, Max was there. She raked her fingers through her hair and thought about screaming, but that would just prove that she really was losing her mind where Max Scalise was concerned.

She changed into heavier boots and went out to her garage, found her snow shovel, and carried it around to the front. At least attacking the snowdrifts would keep her hands busy. Once she finished that, she'd drive out and check on Brody and Megan. Deliver some more classroom materials for the girl. Maybe some craft projects or something.

She almost smiled at the picture in her head of Brody Paine helping out the eight-year-old girl with the Thanksgiving turkeys that Sarah's class had made out of magazines the prior week. The guy didn't strike her as the artsy type.

She cleared the drift that blocked her front door, scraped the snow off her few porch steps, and was halfway down the front walk when she heard his voice.

"You need a snowblower."

Max had followed, after all.

Seven years ago, she'd have given everything for him to come after her. To turn around and tell her that he'd changed his mind. That he'd been wrong. That he didn't have to end things with her.

But that had been seven years ago. Now,

she just wanted him to leave her alone. She dug the shovel's sharp edge into the snow and hefted another load to the side where, in the spring and summer, plants would bloom alongside the walkway in glorious profusion. "Who says I don't have one?" She kept her eyes on the snow as she scraped up another shovelful.

"Why use a shovel if you do?" His black boots crunched on the snow and came into view.

She dumped the snow on his feet. "Sorry," she said without feeling an ounce apologetic. "You're in my way."

He shook off the clumps of sticking snow. "You didn't return my phone call yesterday."

"Was it about Eli?"

She knew it wasn't because his message said only "Let me explain about Jennifer."

"You know it wasn't."

She gave him a brief, pointed look, and wielded the shovel once more. "Unless you're here to talk about Eli, we have *nothing* to say." A few more scrapes and she'd be able to move on to the driveway. If her arms and shoulders held out that long when they were already protesting.

"Fine. I talked to him about the tests."

She exhaled. Beneath her layers of flannel and knit and wool, she was beginning to sweat. "Let me guess. He told you he didn't cheat."

"Right."

"Shocking." Her tone was arid. She pushed the shovel along the cement walkway and it scraped loudly as she cleared away the last several inches of snow.

"He's never lied to me before."

She stomped across the yard toward the driveway. It would take her considerably longer to clear it than the walkway, and the snowblower's appeal was growing. Not that she'd drag it out now, after he'd made a point of mentioning it. She knew that was pretty much cutting off her nose to spite her face, but didn't care.

"You're my son's teacher, Sarah. You have to talk to me."

She tossed the shovel onto the ground where the thick layer of snow cushioned it, and turned to face him, her hands on her hips. "To listen to you, *I'm* your son's problem! You don't want to hear what I have to say when it comes to Eli. You've already made up your mind."

"Sort of like you've already made up your mind about me and what happened between us."

Her lips parted. She was breathless from shoveling, *not* from his presence. "You've got to be kidding me. That's like comparing apples and oranges. For heaven's sake, I'm trying to *help* Eli. And you're just...just sticking your head in the snow!"

He strode across the lawn, leaving fresh footprints alongside hers in the pristine smoothness. "Goddammit, Sarah. I was *not* with Jennifer when I was with you."

She stared at him, wanting to deny the emotion suddenly bubbling over inside her, and being completely unable to do so. "Really." She stomped past him, crossing the yard yet again. "Come with me." She didn't wait to see if he followed as she stormed up the newly cleared steps and porch.

She yanked open the door and went inside, heading straight through to her kitchen. "Look." She pointed at the pile of bows for the ceremony, the favors for the reception. "That's just the stuff I've done in the past few weeks for Leandra's and Evan's wedding. They've been planning it since October, and it's taken most of the family to pull it together in this short amount of time."

Her throat started tightening. "So don't *tell* me that you weren't involved with Jennifer when we were together. I told you. I *saw* the wedding, myself. Events like that don't get pulled together in less than two weeks. I would imagine that you'd had to reserve that particular spot about a year in advance! Am I right? Well?"

His jaw hooked to one side. She couldn't read the expression in his brown-green eyes, but she figured she knew the answer, anyway.

"Of course I'm right." Her voice sounded hoarse. "That wedding probably took six months to plan."

"About nine," he said finally.

She didn't think it would hurt. Not when she was already prepared for the answer; not when she'd reasoned it out for herself all those years ago.

Yet it felt as if she'd been kicked in the stomach.

She reached her hand back for the counter behind her, needing to hold on to something steady. Something concrete.

He yanked off his gloves and shoved them in the pockets of his close-fitted brown coat. "There are things you don't know about it, Sarah. Things I couldn't say. Couldn't tell you."

She just shook her head. "Please, Max. Just go. I can't—I can't keep running into you and going through this. It's over and done."

"But it's not done." He stepped closer. "I wish to God it was."

She took a step back. Bumped into the counter. “Max. Don’t.”

He drew his dark eyebrows together in a frown. “Don’t what, Sarah? Don’t remember? Don’t lay awake at night, still to this day, and want you? Or don’t worry that your judgment when it comes to my son might be skewed because you hate me that much?”

“I don’t *hate* you.” She pushed the words out. How much easier it would be if she did.

He took another step toward her. “But you don’t trust me.”

She couldn’t take a breath without inhaling him. The crispy coolness that clung to his coat. The warmth of his breath. “It doesn’t matter whether or not I trust you,” she managed. “You’re just one of my students’ parents.”

“Liar.” His thick enviable lashes dropped and her lips tingled as if his gaze had actually brushed against them. “I’m your first lover, Sarah.”

She tossed back her head, pride stiffening her resolve. “So I should be quivering in my boots now? Do you really think that you’ve been such a…a *monument* in my life, after just those few weeks we were involved? I could have had dozens of lovers since you. Ones that I tossed aside as easily as you did me.”

"There was no tossing and it sure in hell wasn't easy." His brooding gaze met hers. "And I don't think there have been dozens."

She made a scoffing sound. "It's hardly any of your business now, is it." It wasn't a question.

His head tilted to one side. "How many?" His voice was soft. Impossibly gentle.

"Go to hell."

"Been there. How many, Sarah?"

"How many lovers have *you* had, Max? How often were you unfaithful to Jennifer?"

"That wasn't what our marriage was about."

She lifted her brows, feeling shocked. "Well, how very modern and sophisticated of you both."

His lips tightened a little. "We married because of Eli."

"Oh, well, that makes it all okay then." Her voice cracked. "Did you tell your wife that you had a girlfriend practically up until the week you were saying your vows to each other?"

"She knew about you."

For some reason, that made the edge of pain cutting inside her even sharper.

"She must have been the forgiving type. Unlike me."

"That's not what I meant."

"Then what *did* you mean, Max? You told

her about me after you'd put your ring on her finger? After your honeymoon? After your first anniversary? Or your fifth?" Her eyes burned. "You didn't just go through a wedding, Max. You had a marriage. And until she…she died, you were still together. I wasn't the one who mattered. She was. Your son was. I was just a…blip."

He looked pained and his fingers, when they touched her cheek, weren't steady.

Or maybe that was just because she was shaking. From head to toe.

"You were the one I loved, Sarah." His fingers smoothed down her cheek. Traced her jaw. "That was never a lie."

She had to steel herself not to sink against him. Not to let herself fall into that seductive chasm of believing every word that came out of those perfectly sculpted lips. "Did you regret marrying her?"

"Do you want me to lie now?" He let out a harsh sigh. "I had Elijah to consider. Jennifer was his mother. No. I didn't regret marrying her."

"You loved her."

He let out a sigh. "Eventually. Yeah."

She closed her eyes. Painful or not, at least he had been honest about that. "What do you want from me, Max?"

"I wish to God I knew," he murmured. His finger brushed over her lower lip. Just the slightest of grazing.

She very nearly stopped breathing. She angled her head away, looking up at him again. "I don't get involved with fathers of my students."

"Seven years ago, you told me you didn't get involved with Frowley-Hughes' clients."

"I should have stuck to my conviction."

"Probably." His hand slid back along her jaw, cradling her face.

"And you weren't really a client. I'm not going to get involved with you again."

He lowered his head. His words brushed across her lips like a physical caress. "We're already involved. We have been since the afternoon you talked me into sharing a picnic with you on the beach."

"The picnic was your idea."

"Yeah, so maybe it was." He closed the last few inches between them, covering her mouth with his.

Chapter 6

He tasted of coffee and minty toothpaste.

And Sarah opened her mouth to Max, kissing him back because she couldn't stop herself.

But before she could remember all the reasons why she shouldn't be standing in her kitchen kissing Max Scalise—and they were supposed to be hovering right there in her mind at the ready—he was lifting his head.

She felt like her brain was operating on only half a cylinder when he pulled his radio off his hip and responded.

Naturally. She'd been losing her mind and he'd been perfectly capable of hearing his radio.

She covered her eyes with her hand for a

moment. Then brushed her fingers through her hair. Gathering her composure took effort.

"I have to go."

Her lips twisted. "Of course you do. It's what I've been wanting you to do all along." He wouldn't be leaving just her house, either. Before long, he'd leave Weaver, as well.

She knew it down in her bones.

Max Scalise and the town of Weaver were not destined to grow old together, any more than she had been destined for something other than heartache where he was concerned.

His lips twisted. "Yeah. I noticed that when you were kissing me back."

She felt her face flush. "Look. We're going to have to find a way to be…civil to one another. I don't want my family wondering why—" She broke off and tried again. "They don't know anything about what happened in California. I want to keep it that way."

"Your cousin knows, though. Leandra. Doesn't she?"

She winced. Leandra knew far more than he could possibly realize. "She and Evan will be heading out on their honeymoon in less than a week."

His gaze flicked to the phone that hung on the wall when it suddenly rang. "Early caller."

"That's ironic coming from you, don't you

think? Considering you're standing here in my kitchen at this hour?" She snatched up the telephone. "Hello?"

"Meet me. Two hours." The call severed. And though the voice had been abrupt, she still recognized the caller.

Brody Paine.

Aware of Max watching her, she hung up. "Wrong number."

She was lying, Max thought. *Why?*

But he had his own duties to take care of. Ones he wouldn't shirk.

If there was one thing Max knew about, it was taking responsibility for things.

There were only two people in Max's life that he'd failed. And one of them had just lied, for unfathomable reasons, about the phone call she'd just received.

Indulging his curiosity would have to wait, though. "I'll let you know about Eli's schoolwork if he's not feeling better by Monday."

"Fair enough." Her voice was careful.

Because she didn't want to spar with him over his son's supposed cheating? She sidled past him in the small kitchen and walked through the living room where the delicate, feminine furniture looked almost as if it would break should he sit on it.

Not that he was likely to get an invitation

from her to do any such thing, particularly after he'd kissed her the way he had.

She waited at the door, going through the motions of showing him out, without uttering another peep. The second he was out on the porch, the door shut behind him with a click. "Here's your hat. What's your hurry?" he murmured under his breath, and headed out to his SUV, parked at the curb.

A few hours later, he had just arrived at the new supermarket on the far side of town to deal with a fender bender when he saw the familiar little blue sedan barrel into the parking lot.

He scratched his name on the report and climbed out of his warm vehicle to deal with the annoyed drivers involved in the minor accident. Sarah's blue sedan was still parked in the lot when he finished, and he hooked his radio on his belt, heading toward the entrance of the store.

Inside, the place was fairly bustling. Clerks were stocking special holiday displays, and Christmas music was coming from the speakers. The store hadn't been there when Max had lived in Weaver. It was one of the additions to come after Tristan Clay started up that video game business of his. CeeVid.

Eli had quite a few of the games in his collection.

As proof of its modernism, there was even a small coffee counter near the entrance of the supermarket. The coffee was hot and strong and he bought himself a tall cup of it as he hung around, watching the shoppers.

He garnered as many curious looks as he did friendly smiles, and his coffee was about a third down when he spotted Sarah entering one of the checkout lines behind a tall brown-haired guy and a thin girl who looked about Eli's age.

Sarah wasn't paying much attention to the man—who was unloading his basket for the clerk. But she was giving the girl plenty of it, seeming to be talking a mile a minute. When the guy had paid for his two plastic bags of purchases, Sarah put down her bag of—Max angled his head, trying to see better—flour. It had sure taken her a while to choose one large bag of flour.

She was giving a friendly wave to the girl, who was following the guy right past Max.

He wasn't sure, at first, what made him take second stock of the man as he took the girl's hand in his and left the store. Maybe it was the way the guy seemed to be cataloging his environment as thoroughly as Max was.

From his position near the sliding glass entrance, Max watched the two cross the parking lot. They got into a late-model short bed, parked two spots down from Sarah's sedan.

"What are you doing here?"

He looked back at Sarah. There was probably something wrong in the way he took perverse pleasure in her annoyance. "Drinking my coffee, ma'am."

Her lips firmed and she sniffed. "Too bad they don't sell donuts at the coffee counter, too."

His lips twitched. "Never been one for donuts. Used to leave that for E.J."

Surprise lifted her eyebrows. "You didn't used to mention your partner so easily."

"His death was seven years ago."

"Yeah." She settled her heavy bag on her other hip. "I remember."

He'd have been surprised if she hadn't, considering how messed up he'd been about it. Aside from the departmental shrink he'd been forced to see, Sarah was the only one with whom he'd been able to voluntarily talk about it.

Admitting to her that his partner had caught a bullet during what should have been a routine follow-up on an investigative lead that Max had uncovered hadn't been easy, though. And he'd never been able to admit to her that he'd felt bound to help the ones E.J. had left behind—Jen and Eli.

He jerked his chin toward the bag. "Find yourself in sudden need of flour, did you?"

Her lashes swept down. "I'm making cookies for Thanksgiving dinner, and then for the holiday boutique my school is having next weekend. It's a fundraiser."

"What kind?"

"The money-raising kind," she drawled. "Want to donate something? We sell Christmas decorations and craft projects and all sorts of things. Sell raffle tickets, even. Just got a donation for a weekend stay in Cheyenne's best hotel."

"What kind of cookies?"

"Why? Are you the cookie police now, too?"

"Just curious. Since I'll be sitting down at the same dinner table as you on Thanksgiving."

"You could have declined the invitation, you know."

"And either have to drive somewhere to pick up a decent meal for that day, or poison my own family with my cooking attempts?" He shook his head, belying just how much he'd wanted to get out of it. "No thanks. My favorite is peanut butter, by the way."

Her lips twisted. "I'll be sure to make oatmeal-raisin, then."

He caught himself from grinning. And when she turned around to acknowledge someone calling her name, he thought he caught her fighting one, as well.

She waved to the two boys and their harried-looking mother, then turned back to Max. "Students of mine from last year. Twins. They were a handful in class. Still can't imagine what they're like at home."

"Double the trouble. Who was the guy in line?"

Again, she looked away. "What guy?"

"The one in front of you. With the little girl."

"Oh. Him. They're new in town."

"How recent?"

She shook her head, shrugging. "I don't know. A few months. He's some sort of freelance writer, I think. Doesn't come into town much."

"The girl go to your school?"

"Megan? Not yet." She shifted the flour sack again. "Her dad—Brody—told me that his wife died this past summer. He says that Megan's not ready for school, so he's homeschooling her. That's how I know him. I've, um, given him some school materials for her."

He drained the rest of his coffee and dropped

the cup in the trash bin behind him. "Something going on between the two of you?"

Her cheeks went red. "With who? Brody?"

"Yeah." He reached for the bag. "Twenty pounds of flour seems a lot for cookies."

"I make a lot of cookies and *no*, there's nothing going on between me and Brody Paine. For heaven's sake, I barely know the man." She surrendered the bag to him and sailed out the sliding door.

"There was a time when you barely knew me."

She glared at him. "Consider that to be the foolishness of a twenty-one-year-old." She walked quickly to her car, flipping the collar of her coat up around her neck.

She was tall, but he was a good half-foot taller and he kept up with her easily. "You never did answer me before, Sarah."

She yanked open her unlocked car door, making him think in the back of his mind that she needed a lecture about vehicle safety. She didn't pretend not to understand what he was referring to. "I told you that my love life was none of your business." She grabbed the flour from him and heaved it inside her car. A small puff of white powder shot out of the bag. She muttered an oath and slid behind the wheel, swiping her hand over the passenger seat.

He stepped in the way of the door, preventing her from closing it on him and he leaned down. "Are you involved with someone now?"

She fumbled with her keys, trying to fit one into the ignition. "What if I am? Will that give you reason enough to leave me alone?"

"The only thing that would do that would be a wedding ring on your finger, and I don't happen to see one." With every passing hour, he seemed to be increasingly glad for that fact.

She finally succeeded with the key, and cranked the engine over. "Move away, then, so I can go buy myself one."

The corner of his lips lifted.

She let out an exasperated sigh and rolled her eyes. "Go bug someone else, Deputy. I have things to do."

"Cookies to bake. Peanut butter."

She put the car into gear and he hastily stepped away from the door. But he still saw the triumphant grin she gave when she pulled the door shut and finished backing out of the parking spot.

A moment later, she was buzzing down the row of cars and turning out onto the highway.

He strode to his unit and climbed behind

the wheel. Then he pulled out his cell phone and dialed the sheriff's personal line. "Brody Paine," he said, when Sawyer answered. "I need to know everything there is to know about him."

"Been staying at the old Holley place for a few months. Got a girl he homeschools. Lost his wife recently."

Max added his own comments to the sheriff's. "Where'd he come from? We need the whole story." He described the vehicle he'd seen them use.

"On it." The sheriff hung up.

Max sat there, drumming his fingers on the steering wheel as he watched the comings and goings in the parking lot. The idea that he might one day be investigating drug trafficking in Weaver, of all places, would never have occurred to him even ten years ago.

Now, he knew differently.

Across the United States, small towns were falling prey at an alarming rate. Weaver was merely the latest where he'd been sent. And given his history with the town, he'd been awarded the assignment of uncovering the means that were being used. He hadn't stopped fighting the assignment, though, until his mother ended up in a cast from hip to toe. Send another agent, he'd said, until then. Only there hadn't been another agent available—not in the task force that was already stretched too thin.

His cell phone buzzed. "Scalise."

"Looks like he's off the grid," Sawyer said. "No registrations, no banking, nothing. How'd he cross your path?"

"He didn't." Not yet, anyway. But if there was one thing Max knew, it was that Brody Paine was either on one side of the law, or the other. And no matter what Sarah claimed, there was *something* going on between them.

On Monday, Eli Scalise was back in class.

With a vengeance.

It didn't seem to matter what tack Sarah took with the boy; he was bound and determined to cause mischief.

Oh, he was good at it. She never caught him flagrantly in the act. She didn't actually *see* him smear glue on Chrissy's desk chair. She didn't actually *see* him exchange the lunch meat in Jonathan's sandwich with rubber erasers. She didn't actually *see* him do anything. But by the afternoon recess, her students were practically at each other's throats.

Finally, knowing she was being chicken in not contacting Max, during the kids' chorus practice, she called Eli's grandmother, Genna, and told her the problem.

Genna was shocked. "Max hasn't said a word to me."

Sarah didn't consider that much of a surprise. But she didn't exactly want to get into the reasons why Max thought her judgment was off the mark where Eli was concerned.

"Has he had trouble adjusting to his mother's death?" It wasn't something that had really occurred to her until Brody's panicked call that weekend. Megan, whose real parents had been killed recently, had been giving him fits, yet when she'd met them at their agreed-upon place—the supermarket through which everyone in town eventually passed—she'd seemed perfectly fine and typically quiet to Sarah.

"He did, at first," Genna said. "Jennifer's cancer was so sudden. But Max had him in counseling. I don't think Eli handled the loss in any unusual way, or that he put off grieving his mother. It was over a year ago now."

Sarah sighed. Maybe it *was* something about her that Eli was taking exception to. "Maybe if I talk to Eli outside of the classroom, I might make some headway. I'll call Max and ask if I can bring Eli home today."

"No need to call Max. He's expecting Eli to

come straight to the house after school today. I'll let him know. Perhaps I should talk to Eli."

"Then he'll think I've ratted him out to his grandmother."

Genna made a soft sound. "Well, you have, dear. You do what you need to do, though, Sarah. You have excellent judgment when it comes to your students."

The vote of confidence was more than Sarah had expected. "Thanks, Genna."

"Any time. Let me know how things progress, won't you? Max can be somewhat... closemouthed."

Sarah could well imagine that. "I will. And thanks, again." She hung up.

So, she'd have a short while with Eli outside of the school environment.

What was she going to do with the time?

She wasn't any closer to the answer by the end of the day, when the final bell rang.

"Eli, I'd like you to wait, please."

He shot her a wary look, his backpack halfway to his shoulders. "My grandma's expecting me."

"I know she is. I've spoken with her already."

His lips pursed. He dropped the backpack into the cubby attached to his table and flopped down on his seat. His gaze followed the other children who were making their typical mad dash home for the day.

Sarah waited until the classroom was empty and utterly silent. She didn't look at Eli. She just picked up the erasers that Jonathan had pulled out of his sandwich, and walked over to Eli's desk where she set the items. Sadly, for poor Jonathan's sake, one of the erasers had teeth marks in it.

"I believe these are yours."

He wrinkled his nose, picking up the eraser with the bite taken out of it. "Gross."

"I think so." She returned to her desk and began packing up her book bag. "Fasten your coat. We're going."

"Where?" His tone was suspicious.

As well it might be, given his behavior. "Home."

"You're not keeping me after school?"

"I'm going to walk you home."

His jaw dropped a full inch. "But why?"

"Take a guess," she said dryly.

He groaned a little. He zipped up his parka, though, and shouldered his backpack. "I didn't mean to hurt anyone," he said.

She pulled on her coat, but tossed her scarf into her book bag. Since the snowstorm that had hit, the weather had climbed back up to a more tolerable and usual temperature.

Eli shuffled along beside her as they left the school building. "Don't you got a car?" he asked when she didn't turn toward the parking lot.

"Have a car," she corrected. "And yes, I do. Though I don't need it for coming to school." She pointed across the school yard. "I live over there. Across the street from the park. Students aren't the only ones who walk to school."

"Weird." He squinted, as if the idea had never before occurred to him. And coming from southern California where everyone seemed to drive a car even if it was only for a block, she supposed it might not have.

Slipping the strap of her bag over her shoulder, she pushed her bare hands into the pockets of her coat. "Do you like Thanksgiving time?"

He shrugged. "S'okay."

"It's my favorite holiday."

"More than Christmas?" He kicked his shoe against a mound of snow, scattering it.

"Yup."

"But all you do is sit around and eat and watch football."

"Yes. I can see how it would seem that way." She pointed. "Let's sit on the swings for a sec."

"You're a teacher. Swings are for the kids."

"Well, as it happens, I've been using those swings since I was younger than you." Her voice was droll. "So I reserve the right to still use them when I feel the urge."

He shook his head as if he found her increasingly odd.

She dropped her book bag on a patch of gravel where the snow had melted away, then slipped onto one of the swings. The cold, metal chains screeched at the movement.

She managed not to wince.

Eli, however, found the sound fascinating, for he took possession of the swing next to her and made a point of swinging back and forth, causing a similar noise.

"So, I suppose you know what I want to talk with you about."

He didn't stop swinging. "I guess."

"Eli, I want to help you. I really do. I don't want to see you expelled from school. My goodness, you've only just arrived here."

He didn't reply and she hid a sigh. "You know, your dad thinks that I'm the problem. And if he's right, I'd *like* to make things better." She tipped her toe against the snowy ground, pushing the swing back several inches. The cold chains groaned again.

"That's 'cause you gotta. It's your job."

"Actually—" she lifted her toe and let the swing glide forward "—if I were sticking to the rules of my job, you'd have already been at least suspended."

"Then how come I'm not?"

She dug in her toe again. Pushed back until her toe barely reached the ground. Swayed forward once more. "I don't know. I guess I kind of like you."

"Better 'n the other kids?"

"I like all of my students," she assured him diplomatically. "What was your mom like?"

At that, he shot her a surprised look. "Why?"

"I'm curious."

"*Why*?"

"Because you're my student and I'm interested." *Because your father was married to her.* But she couldn't say that, could she? And she was having enough trouble trying to get to the bottom of Eli's issues without her own emotions being added into the mix.

He let out a sigh much too large for a boy of his size and despite herself, her heart squeezed.

"She smelled good," he said finally. "Like…like summer days."

She let her swing go still.

"Grandma Helene doesn't smell like Mom did," he went on.

Jennifer's mother, Sarah deduced. "Do you see a lot of your grandma Helene?"

"I guess. I spent the nights there when Dad had to work. My grandma here's cool, though. She cooks. Even with her broken leg and all. Grandma 'Lene just orders takeout. Not that there's something wrong with takeout. Mom ordered it a lot, too. You know. 'Cause my dad worked a lot. Before we came here, he usually had to travel a lot of different places."

Sarah moistened her lips. "I imagine you must miss your mother a lot."

His lashes lowered, avoiding her gaze. He pushed the swing a little higher.

"Eli, if I ask you a question, will you be honest answering me?"

His knees bent as the swing sailed backward. "What?"

She watched him swing forward again, and stood from her own swing. When his swing pelted backward, she stepped in the path, and caught the chains when he plowed forward, stopping him midair.

"Cool," he breathed.

She held him there until his eyes met hers. Not necessarily an easy task, because the wiry boy was heavier than she'd have thought. "Do you dislike me for some reason?"

A shadow came and went in his blue eyes. "No." His voice was low.

She believed him.

But not until that moment had she let herself acknowledge how concerned she'd been that his actions *were* about her.

She let out a soft sigh. "Okay." She stepped out of the way, and the swing dipped forward, finishing its arc.

"How come you haven't turned me in to the principal?" His voice was barely audible as he dug his feet into the ground, trying to pick up speed once more.

She eyed him. He straightened his legs as the swing went forward, and put his entire body into it as he swung backward. "Would you have preferred it if I had?"

"Least my dad couldn't ignore that." He suddenly let loose of the chains and sailed out of the swing, jumping to the ground. He landed on his feet, but barely.

"Eli!" She ran over to him, grabbing his shoulders. "Are you trying to give me a heart attack, too?" She crouched beside him, balanced on her heels. "Did you hurt yourself?"

He just shook his head. "I'm fine. All I did was jump."

She looked up to the clear sky. All he'd done was jump, same as she used to do when she'd been a kid, same as she'd seen dozens of other children do. Somehow, it had never made her heart simply stop before, though. "Right. So what do you mean about your dad?"

The faint breeze plucked at the fine blond strands of his hair. "When my mom was around, he used to yell when I got into trouble." He chewed at his lip. "She said it's 'cause he loved me."

"And now?"

He lifted his shoulder. "And now he doesn't care."

"Oh, Eli." She managed not to hug him, though she suddenly wanted to. Badly. "Of course your dad cares."

"He only dragged me here with him 'cause he had to."

"I'm sure he has you with him because he wants you with him."

The boy rolled his eyes. But she caught the glisten in them and knew the uncaring act was completely and totally feigned. "He *is* only here for a while," Eli admitted. "We're going back home when Grandma's leg is better. He said so."

The revelation shouldn't have been a shock

for Sarah, yet it still settled inside her, dark and unpalatable.

"What the *hell* do you think you're doing?"

She jerked and very nearly fell off her heels as the harsh question accosted them.

Max was striding toward them. She could see his SUV parked on the street.

She gave Eli's shoulder a slight squeeze, and pushed herself to her feet. "Max."

He barely spared Eli a glance. "Get in the truck, Eli." He waited until his son was well on his way toward the vehicle before he spoke again. "Care to explain yourself, Sarah?" His voice was tight. Abrupt.

And his eyes were like shards of green glass.

Anger, she hadn't expected. "Eli and I were talking."

"Ever think that you should have consulted his father before you took off with him?"

Her lips parted. She made a point of looking around the wide open grounds of the park. "I hardly consider this *taking off*."

"When you don't have my permission, I don't care if you were just stepping off the parking lot curb at the school."

She winced. "Max, come on. This isn't the big bad city here."

He snorted. "And you think that makes it all right?"

She could have argued. Could have told him that she'd cleared it with his mother—who had his authority yet, to answer for Eli when it came to school matters—but she could see the boy's face from where she was standing.

He'd stopped midway to the SUV and was watching them, worry written in every line.

"No," she said quietly. "You're right, Max. I should have spoken with you first. My apologies."

His eyes narrowed, as if he didn't quite know how to take her abrupt agreement.

She walked over to the swings and picked up her book bag.

When she looked at him once again, this time it was Max who was walking away from her.

Chapter 7

When her doorbell rang later that night, Sarah considered not answering.

But if she didn't, word would get around town quickly enough that she hadn't been under her own roof to answer her door at eleven o'clock at night.

Knowing Weaver's grapevine, she'd soon be battling rumors of a wild, probably lascivious, nightlife.

So she didn't ignore the bell.

She went to the front door and peeked behind the curtained window beside it.

She didn't need the circle of light from the porch light to recognize Max standing on her doorstep.

"Go away, Max." She also didn't need the rumor mill gearing up over the presence of Max Scalise at her house at this hour, either.

Nor was she over the sting of his accusations where Eli was concerned.

"Come on, Sarah. Open up."

"Why?"

She saw him tilt his head back. He exhaled into the cold air, creating a cloud around his head. "Because it's bloody freezing out here."

"Doesn't sound like a good enough reason to me."

He focused on the window where she stood. "So I can eat some crow, all right?"

She pressed her lips together, and pulled open the door.

A draft of cold air slid inside, making her shiver.

He stepped in, his gaze traveling first over her pink flannel robe, then to the chain lock that she very clearly hadn't needed to unfasten. "Start locking your doors," he said flatly. "This one *and* your car."

The day she needed to lock her doors in Weaver was the day something precious would be lost. She closed the door and pressed her back against it, crossing her arms over the chest of her thick robe. "I don't see you spitting out any feathers, Max."

He pulled off his coat, and when she didn't offer to take it, tossed it over the back of her wing chair. Beneath the coat, he wore an aging gray sweatshirt with LAPD printed on the front of it.

Hardly regulation for Weaver, but then the boss man wasn't exactly known for wearing a uniform, either. In fact, Sawyer rarely wore one.

"I overreacted," he said abruptly. "I'm sorry."

The thing was, she wasn't hugely upset that he'd overreacted. Stung, yes. More importantly, though, she was concerned with *why* he'd been so upset. "You were worried about Eli. And you didn't know he was with me," she surmised, watching him closely. "Did you?"

He ran his fingers through his hair, leaving it in short, disheveled black waves. "No."

"Why were you looking for him, anyway? Your mother said you expected him to head straight for the house after school, rather than the station. You were on duty, weren't you?"

"I wanted to tell him I was gonna sign him up for horseback riding lessons."

She raised her eyebrows. "And that necessitated a special trip to school?"

"He's been bugging me about it since we

came to town. We got into it this morning before I dropped him off at school. I left knowing he was upset and I didn't want to wait any longer."

She steeled herself against softening too easily. "As I recall, you don't much care for horses."

He made a noise. "They don't much care for me, is more to the point."

"Then I'll take Eli out riding. Thanksgiving. After dinner. We have plenty of horses at the *C*. You needn't go out and pay for lessons for Eli." She had an idea of what he earned as a deputy sheriff. It wasn't paltry, but paying for something when he didn't have to seemed silly to her. She was a teacher and supported herself. She couldn't pay for too many unnecessary things, either.

"We'll see."

She might not be a parent herself, but she certainly knew what *that* usually meant. *No.*

She decided to let the matter rest. Thanksgiving Day would be there, soon enough, anyway. It would be a simple matter to include a little riding.

"Why would you think someone would take off with your son? Weaver hasn't changed that much since I was a kid. Since *you* were a kid. It's larger, true, but we're still just a small Wyoming town. Everyone watches out for everyone else. Or have you really forgotten that?"

"You haven't seen the kind of crap that happens to people that I have. Whether you recognize it or not, Weaver is not the same town that it used to be," he said evenly. "And I haven't forgotten *anything* about this place."

Which left her wondering what else he *wasn't* telling her.

"I suppose you spoke with your mother."

His lips twisted. "I believe the proper description would be that *she* spoke to me."

"Mmm."

He shook his head and looked at the chintz couch, as if he wanted to sit on it, but was half-afraid to. "She called me Massimo," he muttered. "Believe me. That is *never* a good thing."

She unfolded her arms. Okay. He'd come and apologized for taking a strip off her hide when he'd been worried about the whereabouts of Eli. She should tell him to go.

"You want something to drink?" She nearly slapped her hand over her mouth, but the invitation was already out there.

He angled a look her way. Slightly less surprised than she, herself, felt. "What are you offering?"

Evidently, her head on a platter. “Coffee. Hot chocolate.” Her voice was abrupt. She’d never known him to drink tea, but then she hadn’t known him for all that long.

Just long enough to color everything she’d done in her life ever since.

She pushed her hands in her pockets, crossing her fingers that he’d decline.

“Coffee’d be good.”

So much for childish superstitions. She pulled her hands free. “If I didn’t come from a family of avid coffee drinkers, I’d be shocked at wanting some at this hour.” She pushed away from the door, excruciatingly aware of her state of undress in the face of his softly faded jeans and sweatshirt.

“Sit. The couch won’t fall apart,” she assured. “It’s covered with chintz, not made of it.”

She went into the kitchen, not waiting to see if he sat, or not. She deftly filled the coffeemaker and flipped it on, then stood there staring at the liquid that immediately began dripping into the glass carafe and debated whether or not she should change into some clothes.

If she did, he’d undoubtedly think she’d done so because of him.

Which was true.

She let out a breath, and pulled the sash of her robe tighter around her waist. She was already covered from her neck to her toes, and *those* were covered with fuzzy socks.

It doesn't matter what you're wearing. The voice inside her head was stern. *He's only here because of Eli.*

She fiddled with her sash again. Tapped her fingers against the counter, and willed the carafe to fill more quickly.

"Didn't your aunt once live in this house?"

She whirled. The hem of her robe flew out, baring her knee and she yanked the pink fabric closed. "What?"

His gaze slowly lifted to her face, which felt on fire by the time he reached it. "Your aunt lived here, didn't she?"

"Um, yes. Hope, back before she married my uncle Tristan. He's the one that, um, keeps me supplied in those." She waved her hand absently at the cutting-edge computer sitting on the small secretary desk opposite the stove. Her uncle actually kept the school supplied with computer equipment. The advantages of knowing a man who'd earned a fortune in the business. "And then Belle lived here for a while before she married Cage Buchanan. The place was occasionally rented out to someone outside the family, but not very often."

"Hope. I remember her. Ruby Leoni was her grandmother."

"Great-grandmother, actually. Justine is Hope's mother, not her sister." Evidently, in their day, that revelation had been a bit of a shock.

The coffeepot gave a reassuring gurgle that she recognized as the end of its work, and she grabbed a mug, filled it, and thrust it at him. "There you go."

"Aren't you having any?"

She moistened her lips. Shook her head. It was all she could do not to grab her robe even more tightly around herself. But she figured she already looked uptight enough.

His long fingers curled around the white mug as he studied the liquid. The light overhead picked out the silver strand over his left temple. "What made you turn to teaching?"

She swallowed. That was territory she didn't want to discuss. Not when it was all tangled up with their history. "I missed my family too much. *And* Weaver," she said, which was a good portion of the truth, though not all of it. "Besides which, there's not much call for investment advisors here. For teachers, though?" She managed a faint smile. "Big need for teachers."

Standing there in her minuscule kitchen where he seemed to occupy more than his fair share of the space was making her a little crazy. She slipped past him and headed back into the living room, and took the only single seat there—the wing chair.

He could have the couch all to himself.

Only he didn't head to the couch. He carried his mug in one long-fingered hand as he stopped in the short hallway and studied the framed family pictures that hung on the wall. "Whenever I thought about you, I pictured you living in some glass high-rise, married to another stock jockey."

Her mouth went dry and she wished that she hadn't been so quick to decide against the coffee. She'd convinced herself that he'd *never* thought about her. Not once.

"Are you, um, really happy being a deputy sheriff?"

"I'm here, aren't I?" He lifted the mug to his mouth again.

She recognized well enough that he hadn't actually answered her question. He probably had his reasons for hiding the temporary status Eli had told her about, even if she didn't agree with them.

Max continued looking at the pictures, eventually pointing to one. “Who’s the little kid with Leandra?”

“That was her daughter, Emi. Emily, actually, but we all called her Emi.”

“Called?”

“She died several years ago.”

He blew out a breath. “Must’ve been hell.”

“Yes.” He’d had his share of losses, so he’d certainly know.

“And now she’s marrying Taggart. He’s raising that niece of his?”

“Why do I feel like you already know that he is?”

“You know Weaver. Full of gossip.”

“Yes, and the next round tomorrow morning will probably be about why your unit is parked in front of my house at this hour of the night.”

He finally turned away from the photographs. “Maybe we should give them something to really talk about.”

She stilled.

He smiled faintly, though his eyes were dark and inscrutable. “I’m kidding.”

“Ha ha.”

His lips twisted and a small dimple briefly showed itself in his lean, shadowy cheek.

She deliberately looked away.

"Other gossip around here says you don't go out much."

"Who told you that?"

He grinned slightly. "Tommy Potter, actually. For a deputy, the guy gossips more than any female I've ever known. So?" He finally sat down on the small couch. The feminine fabric contrasted sharply with his masculinity.

"You know how gossip works. Sometimes accurate. Sometimes not." *Why* had she invited him in for coffee? She flicked the long edge of her robe back over her knee which it kept wanting to reveal. A glance at him told her he was perfectly aware of that fact, too. "Gossip about *you* says that you had to come back here because you couldn't find a job anywhere else." Her voice was tart.

"Like you said. Sometimes accurate. Sometimes not."

Frustration nipped at her. "You rarely answer a question straight out, do you?"

Unlike her, he wasn't frustrated, but amused. His lips twitched. "You didn't *ask* a question."

"It was implied."

He smiled. His teeth were straight. White.

And it dawned on her that she hadn't seen him smile, truly smile, since he'd returned to Weaver.

She pulled in a breath that felt a little too shaky. It wasn't fair, the effect the man had. It gave him far too much of an advantage. "Eli." Focus on Eli.

"What about him?"

She flushed. She needed to remember to guard her tongue better. "He…what else is he interested in? Besides horses, I mean."

"Video games, sports and generally making his old man crazy. Once that boy gets an idea between his teeth, he's a dog with a bone."

She pressed her hands together, sitting forward. "Yeah. About that. He, um, well, you know, when he and I were in the park, we were talking and—" She broke off and stood. There was too much nervous energy flowing in her veins to stay still.

"And what?"

She pushed her hands in the side pockets of her robe, only to pull them out again. "Can you believe me when I tell you that I'm… I'm not taking out the past on your son? Eli is so bright. He's imaginative. Creative. He's everything I—" *wanted* "—I like to see in a child. But he *has* been cheating and acting up in class. Badly. And I understand that's out of character for him, so it's hard for you to believe, but—"

"He told me."

She blinked, off balanced by the admission. "He did?" She brushed her hair away from her cheek. "Did he say *why*?"

"He doesn't have to. He's pissed that I moved him here." He sat forward, settling his mug on the coffee table. "So, that's my fault, too."

She closed her eyes for a moment, then moved around the oval edge of the coffee table and sat on the couch, angling toward him. "He's got it in his head that you don't love him, Max."

"No way," he immediately dismissed the idea. "Most everything I've done in this life has been for Eli."

And she'd nursed a broken heart because of it, knowing that Max had chosen Jennifer and their son over her. That the morning after they'd made love for the last time, he'd simply disappeared from her life.

She'd had to track him down, only to learn from a talkative member of his department that he had a son and a fiancée in the wings.

"*You* know that," she said huskily. "Eli, however, has lost sight of it."

His eyes, those changeable eyes of his, focused harder on her face and it felt as if he were looking right through her, seeing directly through all the walls she'd so carefully built against him. "He told you this? Today. In the park. That's what you were doing. Asking my son if he thought I loved him."

"No, I did not ask him that," she said evenly. "I was *trying* to get to the bottom of his behavior in my class. He figures that since you didn't get after him for any of it, that you no longer care about him."

"Where the hell did he get that idea?"

She lifted her palms. "That'll be for you to work out with him. I just thought you should know where his head is at." She dragged her robe back over her knee and pushed off the couch, restlessly moving away from it. "Look, it's late. And you're probably on duty early in the morning and I've got a meeting before school starts, so—"

"Eli isn't mine."

She hadn't heard right. That's what she got for going short of sleep for too many nights. "I beg your pardon?"

He unfolded himself from the couch, too, facing her. His jaw was tight. "I'm not Eli's biological father."

Her lips moved, but no words came. Nothing. Her head had simply gone blank. And her legs felt curiously rubbery. She moved, and when her knee knocked into the wing chair, she sat down on it. "I…see," she finally said. Her tongue felt thick.

"I doubt it." Now he looked the restless one as his long legs ate up the cozy confines of her living room. "He's E.J.'s."

She pressed her fingers against her lips, focusing hard on the two botanical prints framed on the wall above the couch.

"Sarah—"

She dropped her hand, shaking her head sharply. "Why are you telling me this now?" Now, when it didn't matter? Now, when she'd finally put everything—*everything*—behind her?

"I just wanted you to know." He shoved his hand through his hair again. "So that you would at least understand *that*."

But she didn't understand. And the more he told her, the more unclear everything became. "When did you find out?" she asked slowly.

"I knew from the start. Jennifer and I weren't—she was E.J.'s girl."

"You never mentioned her to me back then. Not when you told me about your partner. About his death."

"I know." His gaze was dark. Shadowed. "I should have."

She winced. "So, you *did* have plans to

marry her when we…when you and I…" She couldn't make herself finish.

"I knew what I had to do. Yeah. I hadn't convinced Jennifer of it yet, though." He paused. "That came later. After you."

There was a burning deep behind her eyes. "And the fancy wedding on the beach?"

"Was supposed to have been for her and E.J. She hadn't cancelled all of the arrangements, and it was a pretty easy matter to just use them. Not because she wanted to, but her mother, Helene, was pretty gung ho about her daughter being properly married. Didn't matter so much to Helene *who* the groom was, as long as there was one." His restless pacing ceased for a moment. "I never slept with her."

"Ever?"

He hesitated, looking even more grim. "Yeah, well, later. After we'd been married a while. We were friends, Jen and me. We both lost E.J., though she never blamed me for it. Never understood that it was my lead he was following. If anyone should have been shot, it was me. But she never understood that. In the end, we had a marriage that we both wanted to make work."

"You loved her." She'd figured she'd had a masochistic streak since she'd stood hiding in a bush to watch him wed another woman even after he'd already broken it off with her.

Now she knew the streak had never really gone away.

"Yes. But not at first. Not like that."

Her throat felt like a vise was clamping it shut. She didn't have to ask if he'd grieved her death when she could see it written on his face. "Then why did you *marry* her?"

"I told you. Because of Eli. If it weren't for me, his real dad wouldn't have died, okay? I was E.J.'s partner; I should have had his back."

"Instead, you just had his girlfriend."

He grimaced. "Dammit, Sarah, I told you. It wasn't like that." He scrubbed his hand down his face. "When E.J. was killed, he and Jen already had the wedding planned. That was practically a miracle in itself because they'd had their problems. But they'd worked them out. And they'd put off the wedding as long as they had because Eli was in and out of the hospital back then. He was premature."

He reached the doorway to the kitchen. Turned around and prowled back. "Then, when E.J. was shot, Jen was devastated. She sort of lost it for a while. She was a hairdresser and her insurance benefits were minimal at best; they'd already been pretty much used up with Eli's expenses to that point. Her mom helped where she could, but she had her limits, too.

"E.J. sure in hell hadn't expected to die." His voice roughened. "He hadn't changed his life insurance over to Jen from his ex-wife's name and when he was gone, Jen and Eli were out in the cold. She couldn't even get survivor's support for Eli, because when he was born, she and E.J. were fighting so she didn't put his name on the birth certificate."

"But Eli *was* his son, despite what the piece of paper said. Surely there was some means of—"

"The only means were me," he said flatly. "Believe me. I looked into every other alternative. I'd already been on the force for a while by then. My insurance benefits were completely available, but only to members of my own family. So, I talked Jen into marrying me. After a year or so, I adopted Eli legally as well."

She blinked. A tear slid past her lashes and burned down her cheek. "Why didn't you tell me all of this then?"

"It wouldn't have changed anything. They were the decisions I had to make."

"Then why...why me? Why get involved

with me at all? There was nothing forcing your hand there, Max." And she hated it that she was still looking for something deeper, some reassurance that she hadn't imagined the connection they'd had, something that would tell her that she hadn't been an utter and complete fool.

His pacing brought him closer. "I didn't say they were easy decisions. And you—you were the one thing in my life during that month that *wasn't* all messed up. I wasn't the reason you didn't have the man you loved, I wasn't the reason your baby had no father."

She trembled, feeling a sudden wave of nausea.

"It was selfish of me and I knew it at the time, which was why I told you that first day on the beach that there was no place for us to go. No future."

She'd invited him to that beach picnic. Had wheedled an agreement out of him, because even her virginal twenty-one-year-old self had recognized the look in his eyes when he'd looked at her. He'd confided that he was working a case, and she'd made sure she was there every time he had an appointment with his supposed financial advisor. She'd chased after him until she'd caught him. And when he'd talked about there being no future, she'd confidently assured him that she didn't *care* about the future.

She'd believed his reticence where she was concerned had only been because of what his father had once done to her family.

All she'd cared about was the present. And sharing it with him. Confident in her arrogant innocence that the future would take care of itself.

It had, but in ways she'd never anticipated.

She looked down at her hands, twisted together in her lap until her knuckles looked white. "Does Eli know?"

"That I adopted him? Yeah. He's always known."

"And h-his health issues? What about them?"

"He had a bunch of surgeries. Respiratory stuff primarily. He still has a tendency toward bronchitis that I try to watch out for. But mostly, the older he got, the stronger he became." He stopped next to the chair and bent his knees, crouching beside her.

Her heart stuttered when he covered her twisted hands with his.

He was silent for a long moment. His thumb slowly stroked the sharp ridge of her knuckles.

"Everything I've done since before he was a year old has been for Elijah."

And everything she'd accused him of hadn't been wrong. She hadn't gotten his reasons right, but the end results were still the same.

He'd chosen someone else.

Sarah had still lost their child.

"It's late," she whispered. Seven years too late. "You should go."

In the gentle light of the lamp sitting on the side table beside her chair, his eyes looked so deeply brown they might have been black.

"I'm sorry," he murmured.

Her vision blurred. She pressed her lips together and slowly pulled her hands from beneath his.

"So am I."

Chapter 8

"Happy Thanksgiving!" Assigned to door duty at the Double-C, Sarah stepped out of the way while Max helped his mother maneuver her weighty cast through the wide doorway. "It's good to see you, Genna."

If she concentrated on Max's mother, maybe she'd get through the afternoon without embarrassing herself too badly.

"You too, dear." Genna leaned forward and caught Sarah in a quick hug. "Eli is bringing pies from the car, so beware." She balanced on one crutch while Max helped her work out of her coat. She was dressed in a pretty red sweater and skirt that reached down toward the ankle of her cast.

"Max." Sarah kept her smile in place as she took the coat from him, and waited for him to hand her his own, as well.

It was the first time she'd seen him since that night he'd come to her house. And even though she'd had two and a half days to prepare for the moment, she still found herself entirely *un*prepared.

"Happy Thanksgiving," he murmured. His hands brushed hers as he handed over his shearling coat. His expression wasn't exactly relaxed, either.

If anything, he looked *very* uncomfortable standing there in his dark gray trousers and ivory fisherman's sweater.

More handsome than any man she'd ever seen. But uncomfortable nevertheless.

She clutched the coats to her chest. "Everyone is in the living room. Go on in. Make yourself at home, but beware. Squire is playing bartender, already." Squire Clay was her grandfather. Still standing almost as straight and tall as his five sons, he was opinionated, interfering, and grew more lovably irascible by the year.

She was crazy about the man.

But all affection aside, she knew he could have a heavy hand when it came to pouring a drink.

Genna tucked her crutches more firmly beneath her arms and smiled. “Well, frankly, a drink sounds good to me.” She winked, looking younger than her years, and planted the rubber tips of her crutches to begin working her way through the foyer.

“And that’s why I get to be designated driver,” Max murmured, but at least he’d managed a smile of his own.

A smile that her attention snagged on and they stood there alone, next to the open door for a silent moment that dragged on too long.

He started to lift his hand.

She swallowed and deliberately looked out the doorway that she hadn’t yet closed.

From the side of her vision she saw his hand lower, his fingers curling.

Outside, Eli was slowly making his way through the numerous vehicles congesting the circular drive. His tongue was caught between his teeth as he balanced a pie on each hand.

She couldn’t keep silence up the entire afternoon. “Maybe I should help him.”

“This is a point of manly pride for him.” Max’s arm brushed hers as he looked out, too.

For a moment, she let herself wonder if he’d made the contact deliberately. “Manly pride," she repeated, amused despite herself. "Carrying *pies*?"

"Give him a break. He's eight. And he made those pies with his grandmother. He's not gonna drop 'em."

Eli still had to make it up the half-dozen shallow stone steps to the front door, though. "But—"

"Relax." Max's hand dropped on the back of her neck and even through her turtleneck sweater, she felt singed.

Definitely deliberate.

"He knows to be on his best behavior here," Max said.

She shifted and his hand slid down her spine, then fell away as she looked up at him. "*Here?* What's that supposed to mean?" The Double-C had raised up her father and uncles, then her and her brother and myriad of cousins. It was hardly going to fall in the face of one, sometimes mischievous boy.

"We're Scalises," he said. "This is Clay territory."

As if that should explain it all.

But Eli had made it up the steps by then and any chance she had for a response was lost. "Miss Clay," he lifted the pie tins triumphantly. "Pumpkin and chocolate because

Grandma says no self-respecting woman wouldn't prefer chocolate pie over *squash*."

Sarah smiled and caught the pumpkin pie before it could slip off his flattened palm. "She's right, of course."

"Good job." Max took the chocolate one, and lifted the pumpkin out of her hand. "Your hands are already full," he murmured. "Where should I put them?"

"Um, the kitchen. Through there—"

"Unless it's moved, I remember." He walked out of the foyer and turned to the hall leading to the kitchen that was located at the very rear of the house.

"My dad's been here before, huh?"

"Mmm-hmm. He used to come here sometimes with *his* dad." Though he'd stopped doing that when Tony was arrested. Sarah had been little more than a toddler, then. "You want to give me your coat there?"

He shrugged out of his slick parka and thrust it into her hands. "Dad said you might give me a ride on a horse."

"I just might." Her gaze traveled over his clothing. "But you look quite handsome there in those clothes. Did you bring some grubbies to change into?"

His blond hair was slicked back, still wet from being washed. "Jeans. Dad, too." He looked up at her, as if debating. Then he leaned closer. “I got grounded,” he whispered. “For a whole week. ’Cept for today, he said, ’cause it’s a holiday.”

Never had she heard a boy so happy to be punished. She hid a smile. “I’m glad it didn’t include today,” she admitted.

“Me, too.” His voice was fervent. “You know what else? My dad hates horses. But he said he’d maybe ride.”

She couldn’t help herself. She brushed her fingers through his damp hair, rumpling it a little. “Sounds great.”

Eli nodded and peered around her toward the living room. “There’s a lotta people here, huh?”

“Mmm-hmm. Pretty much my entire family.”

His eyebrows climbed upward. “Holy cra… cow,” he finished, looking innocent. “I only got my dad and my two grandmas. What do you do at *Christmastime?*”

She laughed and took his hand in hers. “We draw names out of a hat to see who we’ll get a gift for,” she said, and watched his expression fall a little at that. “Come in and meet everyone.”

His eyes nearly bugged out of his head when they walked into the merry confusion of the living room. Every piece of furniture, plus chairs that had been dragged in from the dining room, seemed occupied. "Where's my grandma?" he asked.

He was looking at a sea of strangers. She pointed to the couch where Genna was flanked by two of her aunts. "Go ahead," she encouraged.

Sure enough, he made a beeline for her familiar face.

"Cute kid."

Sarah glanced over at her cousin, J.D., who'd flown in from Georgia along with her sister, Angeline, just that morning. "He is."

"That blond hair, he sort of blends right in with the Clays." Her eyes laughed. "Like I do." She wiggled her head and her blond waves danced. Her humor stemmed from the fact that, while blond, she wasn't a Clay by birth.

"He's Genna's grandson. Eli."

"Right. The hunky deputy's boy." J.D. grinned. "Come on, Sarah. You don't think we haven't already heard all about the new pickin's in Weaver? Even if he is getting long in the tooth."

Sarah flushed. "Good grief, J.D., you sound just like Squire. Maybe you're spending too much time with those expensive racehorses of yours."

Her cousin tucked her arm through Sarah's. "Wish they were *my* racehorses," she corrected, "rather than the ones I work with. Then I could retire in a style I'd like to become accustomed to."

"Excuse me, ladies."

J.D. whirled around at Max's voice coming from behind them, taking Sarah with her. "And there he is in person." She stuck out her hand. "I'm J.D. and I remember you, but it seemed like you were a hell of a lot taller."

Max's lips twitched. "Probably because you were a tad shorter back then."

J.D. cocked her head, considering. "Quite possibly. So, how's it feel coming home again? You've been playing out in the waves off California for a spell, haven't you?"

"More or less." His dimple flashed and he turned his attention to Sarah. "And returning has its advantages. Did you make those peanut butter cookies I saw in there?"

Sarah shrugged, feeling suddenly flushed.

"Dad!"

He looked past them to where Eli was boisterously trying to draw his attention. "Pardon me. I'm being paged." He entered the fray, making his way toward Eli.

He really was clearly devoted to Eli. And knowing what she did now, Sarah found herself floundering in a whole new set of emotions. Ones not necessarily mired in the past. Ones that seemed very new and even more frightening.

"Mercy, mercy. He could use those long teeth on me any day." J.D. sighed dramatically. "Lord, but he's a pretty one, isn't he?"

"He's not long in the tooth," Sarah defended. "He's—" She broke off, recognizing the glint in her cousin's eyes that told her she'd walked right into J.D.'s snare.

"I thought so," J.D. whispered, amused. "Hey. Go for it. Celibacy isn't all that it's cracked up to be, and I can testify to it."

"And since when have you been without a man dangling from your fingertips for your amusement?"

J.D. rolled her eyes. "Believe me, you don't want to know how long."

"Honey," Jaimie called to Sarah, "can you check the potatoes for me?"

Sarah nodded, and turned back toward the kitchen. Within minutes, not only was she joined by J.D., but Angeline, Leandra and Lucy—in from New York where she made her living as a ballerina—as well.

They were an eclectic group. J.D. in her blue jeans and white T-shirt that suited her whipcord frame. Angeline in a smoothly tailored ivory suit that disguised her hourglass figure. Leandra—the most petite of them all—wore a sheer, patterned dress that she'd probably found in some funky antique store. Then there was Lucy, who was Cage and Belle's eldest, and generally accepted to be the most elegant of them all. She was living up to expectations in a pencil-slim black dress that only made her look more blond and ethereal.

As different as they all were though, they were family.

Sarah stuck a fork in the enormous boiling pot of potatoes. They were almost tender. She set the fork on the counter and turned to face the crowd.

"Well," J.D. demanded.

Sarah's gaze met Leandra's. She shrugged a little. "Who can control them?"

"Well, nothing." Sarah turned on the oven light and peered in at the turkey that was roasting and sending its delectable aroma throughout the big house.

"Come on," J.D. wheedled. "Everyone in this house knows that man was at *your* house a few nights ago. That particular nugget has kept the phone lines around Weaver buzzing, I'll bet."

"He's Eli's father. My student. We were just discussing him."

J.D. snorted softly. "That ain't all he is, sugar pie. Just one look at those red cheeks of yours is enough to tell us that."

"It's *hot* in here with all the ovens and burners going."

Even Angeline—an E.M.T. who was usually the most serious one of them all—looked amused. "Since when do you conduct parent-teacher conferences at your house at midnight?"

"It wasn't midnight. It was eleven."

"Squire would say to pull the other leg, 'cause it's got bells on," Lucy countered.

Sarah exhaled, exasperated. "What do you want me to say? That we had wild monkey sex or something?"

"Works for me," J.D. said, laughing. "Personally, that's my favorite kind."

"Favorite kind of what?" Gloria, who'd been married to Squire for most of their lives, stood in the doorway, her eyebrow arched.

J.D. muffled her laughter with her hand.

Gloria just shook her head a little, apparently recognizing that she wasn't going to get an answer. "I swear. You girls are every bit as bad as your fathers once were. And you—" she pinned her amused gaze on Lucy

"—obviously let my Belle rub off too much on you."

"I tried, Mom." Belle was poking her dark head around her mother, trying to see into the spacious kitchen. "Anyone seen Nikki around?" Nikki was Belle's twin sister.

"I think she went upstairs to rest for a few minutes before dinner."

Belle turned her gaze upwards as if she could see to the bedrooms there. "Can't believe she's *pregnant*. Forty-four years old. What were she and Alex thinking?"

"Sometimes thinking doesn't have much to do with conceiving," J.D. said abruptly. "I think it's great. I mean, why not? They're happy about it, and we should all be in as good a shape as Nikki is."

"Your sister will be fine." Gloria patted Belle's cheek. "Now, if you're all just going to stand in here kibitzing, then put your hands to good use, and bring some of those trays of appetizers out. And *not* the ones for the wedding reception tomorrow." She turned on her heel and disappeared once more.

"Only this family would have a huge family holiday dinner one day followed by a wedding the next," J.D. muttered, yanking open one side of the enormous stainless steel refrigerator. "So which trays—oh. They're even labeled. Good gravy. Someone's sure organized around here." She began pulling out an assortment of trays, handing them off to anyone who stuck out their hands. Then she took one herself, and nudged the door closed with her slender hip, and headed back into the living room.

Sarah was left in the empty kitchen with Leandra.

"They didn't hear anything from me," Leandra assured.

"I know." Sarah let out a breath. "It's this town. Everyone talks about everything."

"So, how *are* you?"

"Fine." She had no intention of recounting Max's revelations there. "What about you? Nerves calming down yet?"

Leandra nodded. "Actually, they are." Her brown eyes were shining. "I can't wait to marry Evan."

"That's good, 'cause you've got—" Sarah glanced at the clock on the wall "—less than twenty-four hours of singleness left."

"And I'm happily counting off every minute," Leandra assured. "So, do I still need to dislike the man? Because I have to admit, it's not so easy now that he's here in person. He's even helped Evan out with some stuff at the clinic."

"Of course you don't have to dislike him," Sarah said briskly. "Now, go. Take this dip in there. It goes with the veggies that Angel was carrying."

"Yes, Miss Clay," Leandra said in a singsong voice. She took the crystal bowl and sailed out of the kitchen.

Sarah let out a breath.

She could get through the afternoon.

She really could.

"No. I really can't."

Sarah propped her hands on her hips and eyed Max. "You mean you *won't*."

"Same results." He eyed the enormous horse standing placidly a few feet away. "I'm allergic," he said.

She snorted. "Lies like that'll make your nose grow a foot."

"Come on, Dad." Eli was already in the saddle atop Pokey, one of the gentlest mounts the Double-C possessed. He was rocking back and forth in the saddle, clearly anxious to get moving. "You said you'd think about it."

Pokey turned her head toward Sarah and Max, her large brown eyes gentle.

"Even Pokey wants you to saddle up," Sarah encouraged.

"I told you. Horses don't much like me.

I'll watch y'all from here," Max said. Like Sarah and his son, he'd changed into jeans after they'd finished the monstrously huge and decadent meal.

She wasn't sure which she found more appealing.

Max dressed in fine wool, looking urbane and dangerous, or Max dressed in faded blue jeans, looking casual and dangerous.

Either way, *dangerous* was the word she clearly needed to be remembering.

She circled the reins with her leather-gloved hands and urged Donner closer. The horse she'd chosen for Max took a few steps. The reins jingled. The saddle creaked.

The sky overhead was turning gray, and they had maybe another hour or two of light left. "*Why* do you think horses don't much like you? Honestly, I thought it was practically a requirement of Weaver citizenship to know how to ride."

"I didn't say I didn't know *how*." He leaned back against the fence rail.

"When did you ride horses, Dad?" Eli asked. "You never said. How come?"

"I rode horses with my dad," Max finally said. His voice was even, but Sarah could tell that the admission hadn't been one he'd particularly wanted to make.

And, she suspected, he stepped forward and took the reins from Sarah's hand mostly because he didn't want to encourage any more questions from Eli about Tony Scalise. He reached his foot up to the stirrup and grimacing, pulled himself up onto Donner's back.

"Cool," Eli breathed.

Max gave Sarah a wry look. "Yeah, I might need traction after this and he thinks it's cool."

"Push your heels down," Sarah instructed, struggling against the appeal that the man possessed. Max wasn't wearing cowboy boots, but his heavy-treaded shoes possessed a heel of sorts. "Okay." She tapped his shin. "Pull out your foot. I need to let out the stirrups a notch." Her head nearly brushed his leg as she worked the buckle, giving him a little more length. "Try that."

Max stuck his toe through the stirrup again and tried to ignore the proximity of her shining head to his thigh. He could think of about a dozen things he'd rather do than sit on top of an infernal horse—including having a root canal or spending even more hours secretly investigating the backgrounds of every member of the sheriff's department. There was nothing unusual in that job; he'd just never found it quite so distasteful before, looking into the lives of people with whom he was working.

But there was definitely something to watching Sarah moving around him, making sure everything was just so.

"Much better," she said and went around the horse to adjust the other side. She angled a look up at him. "Did you get thrown once or something?"

"Being thrown would have been easier for my ego to take," he admitted. "I was stepped on."

Her eyebrows rose. "Seriously? What happened? Were you hurt? How old were you?"

"'Bout twelve. And hell yeah, it hurt. Damn horse stood on my foot and stayed there for about a month of Sundays. Only ended up with a few broken toes, though," he admitted.

She looked sympathetic and amused all at once. "Where were you?"

"I was working with my dad on the weekends, like I usually did."

"He was a farrier, wasn't he?"

"Yeah." Farrier and convicted rustler. The kind of father every son could be proud of.

Her eyes seemed to mirror the gray of the sky. "So how long has it been since you've been *on* a horse, rather than the other way around?"

"I was fifteen," he muttered. He'd managed to avoid riding completely after his father's arrest and conviction.

She let out a silent whistle. "Wow. We won't go out for very long then. Don't want you getting saddle sore."

"Not from riding a horse, anyway," he murmured.

Her cheeks went red. She avoided looking at him, and checked his hold on the reins. Satisfied that he wasn't completely inept, she headed to her own horse and swung up in the saddle with economic grace. She clicked her tongue, and the beast turned as obediently as a dog, until she was next to Eli. "Okay, kiddo. Remember what I told you about holding the reins?"

Eli nodded. His tongue was caught between his teeth, so great was his concentration.

Watching the young woman patiently explain the basic points of riding to his son, Max shifted and the leather beneath him creaked.

It was an old, nearly forgotten sound.

Just then, though, it wasn't an unwelcome one.

He looked back toward the big, rambling house where Sarah had grown up. She'd been just a toddler when everything Max believed about his father had been shot to hell. When Tony had shown himself to be a thief—and he'd done it while Max sat waiting for him in the truck.

"Earth to Massimo."

He looked back to see both Sarah and Eli watching him, clearly waiting. "Yeah?"

"Ready?" Sarah held up the reins in her left hand.

"No, but that hasn't stopped either one of you from nagging me up onto this nag."

Sarah made a face, but her eyes were sparkling. "Show some good sportsmanship here."

"Speaking of sports, you realize there is a perfectly good football game on that big ol' television your dad has in that house over there?"

"Da-ad," Eli said.

"Fine." He laid the rein against the horse's neck, and sure enough, the animal obediently moved, heading away from the rein. That was one thing that hadn't changed about the Double-C. The horses that the Clays maintained were well trained and responsive as hell.

"We're just going to ride out to the hole and back," Sarah said, bringing up the rear after Eli. "Just keep going straight out from here, Max."

He lifted his hand in acknowledgment. "Straight ahead, Donner."

The horse plodded along and Max looked out over the widespread snow-covered land, beyond the barns and other outbuildings. Mountains in the distance looked blue against the gray sky. A long line of trees stretched toward the horizon, planted to break the incessant wind.

When he'd left Weaver, he'd vowed never to return. Yet here he was.

"What's the hole?" he heard Eli ask behind him.

"The swimming hole," Sarah said. "It's a small lake a few miles out from the big house. We swim there all the time when the weather's warm."

"Not today, though, huh?"

She laughed. "No, Eli. Not today."

Max shifted in his saddle, settling into the horse's rocking rhythm. Sarah's laughter floated on the air. It seemed to curl around him, and for the first time in a long while he didn't feel quite so cold inside.

Chapter 9

"Here." Jaimie Clay pushed several plastic containers of food into Max's hands. "You have to take home leftovers. A requirement of eating Thanksgiving Day dinner with us."

"That, and if we used up every refrigerator this family possesses, we wouldn't have room for all the leftovers," Sarah said, smiling crookedly.

Max handed off the containers to Eli, whom he'd had to practically tear away from Hannah. The little girl was half his age, and somewhat remote with nearly everyone—a result of her autism, he assumed. But she'd glommed onto Eli the moment they'd reentered the big house after putting up the horses from their ride.

Not that Eli had seemed to mind. Aside from him, Hannah was the only other youngster present; the other young people were all at least of driving age.

"Take those to Grandma in the truck," he told his son.

Eli nodded and turned away, jumping down the steps, only to stop midway. He turned and looked back. "Thanks for letting us come to dinner," he said. "It was real nice of you."

"You're very welcome," Jaimie said, smiling. "It was real nice of you to come and join us." Her green gaze followed Eli down the rest of the stairs and back through the throng of vehicles that gleamed under the illumination from the porch light. "Your son is delightful, Max." She squeezed his arm. "Now, we'll see you tomorrow at the wedding, won't we?"

"Think I'm on duty, ma'am."

"Ma'am. Oh, save me from that, please. Call me Jaimie. And if you won't tell Sawyer that you need to be available for our big do, then I will." She glanced back toward the house when someone called her name. "Sarah, you talk to the man." Smiling again, she went back into the house, closing the heavy door behind her.

Which left Max standing alone under the porch light with Sarah.

She'd pulled an oversized plaid jacket over her shoulders. Her hair hung loose over her shoulders, the ends lifting in the whispering breeze, like beckoning fingers.

And he could have sworn he saw a twitch of the lace curtains hanging in the enormous window that overlooked the front of the house. "Are we being watched?"

She didn't look back at the window. "Probably. Couldn't begin to tell you by whom, though. Any one of those people in there is capable of it." She leaned her shoulder against the pillar closest to the steps. "Don't let my mother make you feel pressured to come to the wedding," she said. "If you're busy or… whatever." Her voice trailed away.

"Would you prefer it if I didn't show up?" Aside from a few awkward moments, the day had gone better than Max had expected. During the horse ride, she'd even seemed to enjoy herself, though she'd kept her attention mostly on Eli.

"I'm just part of the wedding party," she said blithely. "It's nothing to do with me."

He snorted softly. "Bull."

Her lips firmed. "Your mother's planning

to be there. Go with her if you want. If you don't...well, don't go."

He turned his back on the lacy window, blocking Sarah from the view as well. "I want to know what *you* want, Sarah."

Her lashes dipped. "Max—"

"Yes or no. Toss a coin if you have to."

She sucked in her lower lip for a moment, leaving it with a soft shine that seemed to catch the light as much as it did his gaze. Her fingertips were pressed lightly against her throat. "Yes," she finally whispered.

He felt like he'd just cleared a fifty-foot hurdle. "Eli had a good time today. So did my mother." Because he didn't really give a good damn about who was watching from behind the curtains, he touched those flirting tendrils of hair.

Silky. Just like he remembered.

Her lips parted and he heard her soft breath.

"I had a good time today, too," he admitted.

"Good." Her voice was husky.

He looked beyond her. The SUV was running, the exhaust making clouds in the colder air. His mother sat waiting in the front seat. Eli in the rear.

Some things should be simple. Like standing on a porch, bidding your goodbyes to a pretty girl after a nice day.

But nothing was simple about Weaver, nor about Sarah. Not then. Not now.

He let her hair slip free of his fingers. "See you tomorrow."

She nodded, and he felt her wide-eyed gaze on him as he went down the steps to the SUV.

"I now pronounce you husband and wife."

Cheers filled the cozy church as the minister made the announcement. Smiles wreathed his weathered face as he continued, though they held nothing on the smiles the bride and groom were giving each other. Leandra, in her buttercup-colored gown, looked like a breath of spring next to her tall, tux-clad, black-haired groom.

"Ladies and gentlemen, it's now my pleasure to introduce to you Dr. and Mrs. Evan Taggart."

Sarah didn't bother hiding the tears in her eyes when Leandra turned and took her bouquet of lush lilacs back from her. A moment later, the couple was heading up the center aisle toward the exit of the crowded church.

Leandra's brother, Axel, had served as best man. He grinned and gave Sarah a wink as they moved next to each other to continue the recessional. "Now we can get on with the partying, right?"

She chuckled, nodding. But her gaze kept wandering over the congregation who were now all on their feet.

Max's face wasn't among them.

He hadn't come, after all.

And the disappointment of that fact ran alarmingly deep.

The church wasn't really large enough to hold all of the people who'd turned out to see the nuptials. Those who hadn't made it inside, stood crowded around outside, despite the crisp, cold evening. Before Leandra went out the wide-opened doors, she stopped and collected the thickly lined cape that matched her gown and swung it around her shoulders.

Tabby, who was the other bridesmaid, followed closely behind Sarah with Sarah's little brother, Derek. Though, at twenty-four he was nowhere near as little as eighteen-year-old Tabitha, and Sarah gave him a pointed look when she saw his appreciative gaze lingering on Tabby as she handed the younger girl the cape that matched her lilac-colored dress.

"Thanks." Tabby swung it around herself and managed to look even more striking with her black hair against the lovely wool. "Probably looks better than the parka I have in my car." She grinned and without a second glance at Derek, headed out toward her own buddies—primarily Caleb Buchanan and April Reed.

"Put your eyeballs back in your head, Derek," Sarah murmured. "She's too young for you."

"She's eighteen, isn't she?" But Derek didn't seem unduly crushed. Particularly when two women that Sarah couldn't quite place rushed up to him, ostensibly to keep him warm as they pressed themselves against him.

Leandra and Evan were already shaking hands and greeting people. They had decided that Hannah would be too upset by the crush of unfamiliar people; she was already at the home of her grandmother, Sharon, who would be watching her until Leandra and Evan returned from their brief honeymoon. As soon as the bridal couple could break free of the people crowding around them, they'd all head to Clay Farm, where the reception was being held.

"When you gonna let your old man walk you down the aisle?" An arm suddenly came around her shoulders.

Sarah leaned her head against her father and smiled. "Think there was a day when I wanted to marry you, but mom told me you were already taken. Afraid finding someone up to that par has been difficult."

His eyes crinkled. He brushed his lips over her forehead. "The par is off the charts because of you," he assured. "So, what's going on between you and Scalise?"

She stilled. "Nothing."

"You sure?" His eyes were sharp as they focused on her face. "Didn't seem that way yesterday out at the big house."

"You've said that about nearly every unattached man who's come into my vicinity since I was five," she reminded him, keeping her voice light. "I remember when I was in high school, you used to sit on the porch cleaning your shotgun when it was time for one of my dates to pick me up."

"Worked, didn't it?" He looked unrepentant.

"Too well. Half of my class was afraid of you."

"As it should be with a pretty girl's father." His lips twitched. "But now, well, you know your mother's making noises about grandbabies. Says it's been too long since we've had little ones running around the house."

"Don't let him kid you." Jaimie came up beside them. "He wants to hear the patter of little feet just as much as I do."

"Come on, Red, don't blow my cover here."

"Oh, you love it." Jaimie reached up and

lightly kissed his lips. "Now, come on. We can't dawdle around here. People will be heading out to the farm and I promised Emily we'd be there to greet folks since they'll be tied up here for a while with the receiving line."

"You riding out with us?" Matthew looked at Sarah.

She shook her head. "I'm going to make sure we don't forget any of Leandra's things behind in the bride's room. Plus there are some wedding presents I still need to load in my car. I'll be along as soon as I can, though."

Satisfied, her parents moved off.

Sarah's gaze traveled over the throng once again.

Still no Max.

She slowly worked her way through the crowd, exchanging greetings as she went, until she made it to the parking lot where cars were already jammed, trying to get out of the single exit.

The only sheriff's department vehicle around was her uncle's.

And then, because she felt foolish standing in the parking lot for no discernable reason, she went to her car and unlocked the trunk. Gifts of every size and shape were already inside. Despite Leandra and Evan's request for no gifts, people were still bringing them anyway.

Leaving the trunk wide, she went in through the rear entrance of the church and began loading up the gifts that people had left in the narthex. Some of her cousins eventually appeared, helping, and before long, the gifts were all packed, the parking lot was nearly cleared, and there was hardly anything left for her to do at the church. Leandra and Evan departed and Sarah sent everyone else on ahead to the farm.

She went back inside the church, making one last pass, even though she'd already gathered up every last gift, every last flower petal. Now, all she found was one forgotten gold, silken bow with the wild heather attached.

She picked it up, twirling it between her fingers.

The sun was still above the horizon, and it cast its angled beam through the stained glass window behind the pulpit, throwing the colored panes into sharp relief.

The church was small, and probably half of her relatives had been married or baptized in it.

There was even a time when Sarah had dreamed of walking down the center aisle, carrying her own bouquet of wildflowers.

She shook her head at the sentimental thought. She had a teaching career that she thoroughly enjoyed and a calling in her role with Hollins-Winword that she believed in. She no longer had the notion that "happily ever after" existed for everyone.

If it did, she'd have a child only a little younger than Eli.

Instead, all she had was her involvement with other peoples' children.

"Guess I missed the vows."

Her fingers tightened around the bow, crushing the heather. She slowly turned on her heel.

Max stood at the narthex doors. He wore a black suit, but his dark red tie was unknotted, hanging loosely around the neck of his white shirt. "So, a funny thing happened on the way to the church," he said.

She managed a faint smile. "I think that only works when you're the groom who is late."

He tilted his head in acknowledgment and slowly headed into the sanctuary. When he reached the last row of pews, he dropped his hand on the wooden arm. "I saw your car in the lot outside."

"I was just, um, seeing if we'd forgotten

anything." She lifted her shoulders a little, and held up the bow. "This is it."

His fingers grazed over the next pew as he slowly continued toward her. "I *was* headed here."

"The tie was my clue."

His lip twitched. "Yeah." He pulled one end and it slid out from beneath his collar. He rolled the tie in a ball and tucked it in his pocket. "Something came up that I had to take care of."

"Your mom didn't make it," she said, hoping he would elaborate.

"She was tired after yesterday. Her leg was giving her fits. Eli stayed home with her."

She waited, but he said no more about what had kept *him* away.

"Nice dress."

Feeling self-conscious, she swept her hand down the lilac gown. "This old thing? Just something I found in the back of my closet."

His gaze worked its way up to her face. "You look good in anything."

Her fingers tightened on the bow. It crinkled softly.

"And in nothing," he finished.

She stared at him, unable to think of a suitable response to save her soul.

But his gaze went past her to the pulpit and

the high stained glass windows she'd been studying. "Lightning's probably gonna strike me down now."

She moistened her lips. "Well. This *is* a church."

"Except I do think God knows about what goes on between men and women."

She couldn't argue that particular point. "I, um, I need to go."

"The reception?"

She nodded and started to turn, lifting her long skirt with one hand.

"Save me a dance."

She stopped. The dress swished as she shot him a quick look. "You're going?"

He didn't stop his approach, closing the distance between them to only two pews width. "I was invited, wasn't I?"

"Yes, of course," she said slowly.

"Then don't look so surprised."

"Everything about you lately surprises me."

He finally stopped when the toes of his black shoes were brushing the hem of her dress. "That makes two of us."

He must have shaved again since morning, she thought dimly. Because his lean cheeks were still smooth, no hint of five o'clock shadow.

"Max—"

He drew his dark eyebrows together when she said nothing more. "Sarah."

She swallowed. She didn't know what to make of the man. For that matter, she didn't know what to make of herself. She was supposed to have him all neatly boxed up and categorized.

He reached up and she nearly jumped.

But all he did was draw a small spray of baby's breath from where it was tucked in her hair. He brushed the tiny, delicate white blossoms down her cheek. "You need your car there?"

"Hmm? Oh. Yes. G-gifts are in the trunk."

His lashes drooped until there was nothing showing of his eyes but a narrow, brown gleam. "I'll follow you, then."

She managed a nod. "Right. Okay." She turned on her heel, feeling absurdly unsteady, and made her way through the back of the church to the door there.

When she looked back, Max was not following her.

But when she climbed behind the wheel of her car, trembling as if it were thirty degrees below the zero mark rather than above it, she saw him sitting in his SUV, idling in the street.

She flipped on her heater and headed out of town toward the farm.

Max didn't budge from her rearview mirror the entire while.

When they arrived, the sun had nearly set and there was an even larger crowd hanging out beneath the enormous tent that had been erected directly in front of the house. Dozens of propane heaters were burning, keeping the cold mostly at bay. A country-western band was situated on the wide, rambling porch, already playing.

Sarah pulled her car around to the rear of the house, but there was simply no hope of parking very close. Not with that many vehicles.

Max parked beside her and when she opened her trunk, he nudged her toward the house. "I'll get 'em," he said. "You just want them inside the house?"

She nodded, still hovering.

He lifted his eyebrows. "You'd rather hoof all these inside yourself?"

"No."

"Then go. I'll find you."

She went. Straight into the house and to the first empty bathroom she could find, where she closed the door and leaned back against it, shaking like a leaf.

But hiding in the bathroom at her cousin's wedding reception was hardly the mark of a controlled woman, and eventually, she had to force herself to leave the temporary sanctuary. She tightened the sparkling clip that was holding her wavy hair more or less under control at the back of her head and the remaining sprig of baby's breath fell free.

She moistened her lips, picking it up.

Oh, Sarah. Keep your head, girl.

She dropped the tiny spray in the trash and quickly splashed water over her wrists. Then she yanked open the door to brave the world.

J.D. stood there in the hallway, a sly smile on her face. "Hiding out?"

Sarah made a face and swept past her cousin. "Not in this lifetime."

J.D. laughed and took possession of the powder room. "Sell it somewhere else, honey."

There were people everywhere Sarah turned as she made her way back downstairs. She stopped in the kitchen, only to be shooed out by her aunts Maggie and Hope, who had the place well under their control.

She finally pulled her cape around herself and went back outside.

And despite the hundred or so people who were crowded under the tent, she spotted Max immediately. Standing next to the table where an enormous barrel was holding bottles stored in ice, he was holding one of the beer bottles and talking with Sawyer.

She wondered if it was only in Wyoming that people could drink icy beer outside on a winter day.

The lead singer of the band was talking, introducing the new bride and groom, who were occupying the center of the wooden dance floor that was set up in the middle of the linen-draped tables. A moment later, they began playing again and Sarah dragged her gaze away from Max to watch her cousin dance with her brand-new husband.

Within minutes, the couple's parents had joined them on the dance floor.

Angeline came up beside Sarah. "Pretty romantic," she said with a soft smile. "Remember when we were little and took turns playing bride?"

"I think our veil was usually one of the dish towels from the kitchen that we held on with hair bands."

"Come on, sis. I'll dance with you." Casey joined them. He, too, held a beer bottle in one hand.

Angeline just eyed her not-so-little brother. "Since when do *you* know how to dance?"

"Hey. I've learned all sorts of things that you don't know about." He grabbed her hand and pulled her unceremoniously toward the dance floor.

The prickling at Sarah's nape told her Max had come up behind her before he spoke. "You've got a nice family," he said. "Here." He handed her a glass.

She looked at it.

"It's grapefruit juice," he said. "Only juice. Kept Squire away from it, though he was plenty willing to spike it if that's the way you want it."

Sarah took the glass. "This is fine. Thank you." She sipped at it. The last thing she needed was to add alcohol to her already shaky resistance.

"How many *are* there of you?" His arm brushed her shoulder as he lifted his bottle for a drink. "That dance floor's nearly full and I don't think anyone but your family is on it."

"Let's see. Starting with Gloria and Squire—" she mentally counted "—more than thirty, actually. We could do a head count, actually. Ryan's the only one not here."

"Sawyer's boy."

"Yes." Though Ryan was thirty-three and hardly a boy. That wasn't keeping the entire family from worrying about him, though, as his absence continued.

"Well. Come on."

Her fingers felt slippery on the glass. "Where?"

"So cautious," he murmured. "When did that happen?"

She didn't answer and he made a soft noise. "More things to hold me accountable for." He took the glass out of her hand and set it on a bare space on the table behind them. "The dance floor," he said. "Think there's a rule somewhere that says the maid of honor has to be on the dance floor." He held out one hand, palm upward.

She looked at the square palm. The long fingers.

And even though she was afraid she was making the biggest mistake she'd made in recent years, she slowly settled her hand on top of his.

Chapter 10

Later, Sarah could hardly recall any details of the reception. It was a blur of sparkling lights and music and voices. And at the center of it was Max.

Max, who kept her locked in his arms on the dance floor just long enough to drive her slightly insane before he'd surrendered her back to her maid-of-honor-type duties. Tasks that she must have managed, though as she was driving her car home hours later, she couldn't even remember.

Still, she had the bridal bouquet sitting on the seat beside her.

Somehow or other, she'd ended up catching the thing when Leandra had tossed it.

And after the cake and toasts there had been more dancing, during which the magnetic focus of her personal compass had been called away on some sheriff's department matter.

Max's departure had been just as well.

Things were getting just too foggy where he was concerned.

"Distance is a good thing," she said aloud, then laughed a little at her own absurdity. She flipped on the radio station and turned the heater up a notch. The temperature had magically held out for the wedding and reception, but according to Sarah's dad, another snowfall was on its way.

And everyone knew that Matthew Clay had a nose for snow.

The familiar road swept out before her in an unending lazy arc and she reached out with one hand, brushing her palm over the soft petals of the bouquet. Suddenly the car lurched and she jerked the wheel, sucking in a gasp as she bumped over the shoulder.

The car rocked to a jolting halt and she winced as her seatbelt forcibly restrained *her* rocking, as well.

She pressed her head back against the headrest, catching her breath. The bouquet had tumbled onto the floor, but that seemed the only casualty of her precipitous stop. The engine was still running; a jazzy sax was still crooning on the radio station; the heater was still blowing out warm air; the headlights were still beaming out over the road—albeit at a lopsided angle thanks to the car's position.

She unclipped her safety belt and climbed out of the car and the cause of her problem was immediately apparent in the sight of her tire, laying in pieces still on the highway. "Great." She pulled her cape closer around herself and climbed back in the warmth of the car.

She had a spare in the trunk, of course, but the idea of changing it held about as much appeal as sticking her head in a vat of motor oil. Calling a road service would be fine, only it was about two in the morning. By the time somebody made it out to assist her, she could have the spare on herself.

Only a day earlier she'd had an extra pair of jeans in the car that she could have slipped into. But she'd emptied it of all unnecessary items to make room for wedding paraphernalia. Grumbling under her breath, she turned the steering wheel until her tires were straight again, and hit the button to pop open the trunk. Then, she got back out on the shoulder, pulled on her cape, fastening it snuggly around her neck, and went to the rear of the car to unearth the jack and lug wrench.

She had the lug nuts loosened and the car up on the jack when headlights swept over her. She squinted into them, unable to see beyond the glare, but wasn't surprised when the vehicle pulled over to the side of the road behind hers.

That's what people did in those parts.

She lifted her hand in acknowledgment as the driver climbed from the vehicle, and kept twisting the jack, lifting the car another inch.

"Now there's a sight," a familiar voice said.

She squinted into the light again, surprised. "Brody? Is that you?"

"In the flesh." The man walked up beside her and crouched down next to the car. "Having fun?"

She snorted softly. "Barrels of it."

"Here." He nudged her hands out of the way on the jack.

She was happy enough to scoot out of the way. "Where's Megan?"

"Sound asleep in her bed," he assured. "Had to take care of another matter this evening. An associate of ours is with her."

An associate. She rolled her eyes at the term. In minutes, the tall near-stranger had the tire off and was fitting the spare in place. "So, you always get dressed up to change tires on the highway in the dead of night?"

"Doesn't everyone?"

He laughed softly and let down the jack. The car's weight settled once more on all four tires and he tightened the nuts. "Okay, kiddo. You're good to go." He dropped the remains of her ruined tire in her trunk, tossed in the jack and wrench after it, and closed the trunk.

"Thanks. You came by at the perfect time."

"Well." He leaned down and twitched her ankle-length cape. "Nearly."

Sure enough, she had a lovely black mark crossing the front. But at least it had occurred after the reception rather than before.

"You gonna be okay now?"

She nodded. "Of course. These are my stomping grounds, remember?"

"That's what I hear." He lifted a hand and was striding back to his vehicle when another set of lights swept over them.

This time, Sarah recognized the vehicle immediately.

Particularly when he turned on the light bar atop the SUV, and red and blue lights slowly flashed over them.

"What's going on?" Max asked, approaching. He looked very much in deputy mode, she thought vaguely. He neared Brody and the two men gave each other a sizing measure.

Sarah shivered and pulled her cloak closer around her. “I had a flat tire,” she said and her voice sounded loud in the night air. “He stopped to help me change it.”

“And you would be?”

Brody stuck out his hand. “Brody Paine,” he said shortly.

Max ignored the hand and kept walking toward Sarah. “You all right?”

“Of course.” She thought she heard Brody cover a snicker with a cough. For a high-priced agent he was hardly subtle.

“I’m gonna head out, since you’re in such good hands,” Brody told Sarah. “That all right with you, *Officer?*”

Max’s head slowly turned and he gave the man a long look. “You can go,” he finally said.

Sarah pressed her lips together, not sure if she was amused or irritated at the display of testosterone flying between the two males. She turned and climbed into her car, cranking the engine over.

The air that shot out of her heater vents was lamentably cold, though. It would take a while to heat up again. She leaned over and caught the bouquet off the floor, setting it back on the seat.

Max knocked on her window and she rolled it down. Brody's pickup was moving back onto the highway, giving them a wide berth before picking up speed.

"Supermarket guy also performs roadside assistance, does he?"

She stiffened a little. "They do around small towns like Weaver."

"Kind of coincidental."

She flapped her hands. "It's a small town! Now, do you mind if I get moving? It's cold and late."

"Not at all."

He stepped back from the car and she rolled up the window.

Her hands were shaking.

It was as if the man who'd moved with her on the dance floor had never existed.

She punched the gas a little harder than necessary, and her car shot off the shoulder with a spurt of dirt and gravel. In her rear-view mirror, the emergency lights atop Max's vehicle were doused and a moment later, his headlights were beaming into the mirror.

She adjusted it so the lights weren't blinding her, and continued driving into Weaver. When she passed the sheriff's station, she fully expected him to pull into the lot beside it, but those headlights of his stayed steady and strong in her rearview mirror.

He followed her right up to her house, pulling around in the back where she parked near the door.

"You needn't have followed me all the way here," she said, climbing out of her car. "As you can see, the car was just fine once the tire was changed. *I'm* just fine."

He joined her on the steps leading into the kitchen and cursed under his breath when he twisted the knob and found it unlocked. "What'd I tell you about your locks?"

She brushed past him and went inside, unwinding her cape as she went. She left it sitting on the washing machine and slapped on the wall switch as she passed it, throwing the kitchen into bright light. "Interestingly enough, I can choose whether to lock my doors or not." She rounded on him, her hands on her hips. "What are you doing?"

"My job," he said, his lips twisting. "Watching out for the citizens of Weaver. Do you have any idea how dangerous it is to stop on the road like that? Particularly at this hour?"

She lifted her eyebrows. "You happen to notice that I had a *flat?* What was I supposed to do? Drive the rest of the way into town on my rim? And Brody Paine was just being a good Samaritan. You didn't need to act so suspicious of him."

"Honey, I'm suspicious of any man who comes around you."

Her lips parted. Annoyance clogged her veins, making her face feel hot. "Just because we shared a few dances tonight doesn't mean you can—"

Her words caught in her throat as he grabbed her shoulders and pulled her close. "I'm going to kiss you," he said flatly. "Say no, if you really mean it, and I'm out of here."

He waited, his gaze darkly brown.

She opened her mouth. But the word *no* simply did not emerge, though every logical, functioning brain cell she possessed was screaming at her to say the word.

"That's what I thought," he muttered, and lowered his head.

She barely had time to draw breath before his mouth covered hers.

Hot. Desperate.

She wasn't sure if that stemmed from him or from her. All she knew was the taste of him.

Familiar, yet new.

And it was a lot more enticing than those logical cells in her brain.

His hand caught her face when he finally lifted his head. His breathing was rough.

Hers was no better.

"I'm sorry," he muttered. "Sorry."

She touched the tip of her tongue to her lips that felt swollen and tingling. "Really?"

His jaw cocked. She saw the edges of his teeth come together. "No. Not really."

Her hands snaked up around his neck, fingers sliding through his thick hair. "Thank goodness," she whispered and pressed her mouth to his jaw. She slowly touched the tip of her tongue against the rough stubble there.

His hands caught her waist again, fingers flexing. "I didn't intend this."

Such horribly, horribly familiar words when they came from him.

And still she ignored the common sense that cried out for her to run.

Run far.

Run fast.

But most of all…run.

"Yet here we are," she said huskily. "Again."

His hands slid up her spine. "You can always say no, Sarah. I'm a bastard, but I don't push that line. You want me to go, I will." He looked pained. "I won't like it, but I will."

What was worse? Being miserable that

she'd sent him away? Or being afraid of letting him stay?

"I want you to go," she whispered huskily.

A muscle worked in his jaw. He slowly drew his hands away from her back.

She felt cold.

He headed for the kitchen door. "Lock this after me," he said evenly.

She swallowed.

His hand closed over the knob.

He was really going to leave.

She crossed the room, stopping him with her hand atop his. "Max. Wait."

He let out a harsh breath. "I'm a little short of control here, Sarah."

She slowly slid between him and the door, facing him. She dragged his hand to her mouth and pressed her lips to his palm. "Sometimes control is overrated."

He pulled his hand away, pressing it flat against the door above her head. His gaze was fierce as he studied her for a long, tight moment.

Then he lowered his head until his lips grazed her earlobe. "I've never stopped wanting you."

She let out a shaky breath, her eyelids suddenly feeling heavy. Her fingers climbed up his chest, slid over the solidness of his shoulder, still clad in the suit coat he'd worn for the wedding. Found his neck and kept sliding until they tangled in his thick, thick hair. "Max—"

He tilted his head back against her touch, like a big, dangerous cat. His gaze burned over her face and he reached for the single narrow strap of her dress, tugging it down over her shoulder.

She tucked her tongue between her teeth, biting down to keep from moaning right out loud.

His fingers traveled over her bare shoulder, slipping behind to slowly walk down her spine. "Where's the zipper?"

She could hardly breathe. She drew his hand back over the front of her shoulder, nearly seeing double as his palm brushed over her breast, but she didn't stop, continuing to guide him beneath her arm to the hidden zipper in the side of her dress.

He slowly drew it down and the fabric fell away, revealing the strapless corset she wore beneath.

He made a strangled sound.

She felt her skin flush, from head to toe. "It was the only thing I could find to wear under this dress that didn't leave a line showing."

He laughed gruffly. "Believe me, darlin',

I'm not complaining. Just would've been good to have some warning. I think I might be having a heart attack here."

Flushing even harder, she pushed out from beneath his arm, only he caught her from behind, hauling her right back to him.

His lips covered the point of her shoulder. "Don't go running scared now, Sarah."

"Who said I was scared?"

His palm flattened against her abdomen and he slowly, deliberately nudged her dress over her hips.

It fell in a pool of lilac silk around her ankles.

"Maybe I am," he murmured, his words a caress against her skin.

"What have *you* got to be scared about?" She tried not to groan when his hand crept upward, brushing against her breasts, snugly confined within the ivory fabric.

"Same thing as always where you're concerned." His fingertips dragged along the straight edge where corset gave way to soft flesh. "Forgetting everything else that suddenly seems less important."

"And that's bad."

His palm flattened against her collarbone, fingers nudging her head back against his shoulder. "That's dangerous," he murmured.

He turned her head until his mouth touched hers. He slowly sucked in her lower lip, then released it.

She twisted around to face him, only to realize her feet were still caught in the folds of the dress. She kicked at it, trying to step free.

"Definitely a heart attack," he muttered, falling down to his knees. He caught her ankle in one hand and lifted her foot from the fabric.

She grabbed his shoulders, as much unbalanced by his hand on her ankles as she was by him lifting her foot.

When he pulled the dress from beneath her other foot, he didn't rise, though. His fingers slowly slid along the very narrow strap that circled her ankles until he found the minuscule buckle.

She held her breath, watching him as he carefully worked the strap free and turned to the other one.

"Lift."

She raised her foot again and he slid the fancy pump free.

Suddenly a good three inches shorter, she almost wished for the artificial height back. Something about being closer in height to him had given her a foolish sense of confidence that was now completely, frighteningly absent.

His hands drifted up the backs of her calves. Her thighs. Skimmed over the garters holding up the fine weave of her nude hose, and far more easily than she'd fastened them earlier that day, he released them.

His head tilted slightly, looking up at her as his hands continued upward, settling around her waist.

J.D. didn't have it even half-right.

Max wasn't pretty.

He was the most beautiful man Sarah had ever seen in her life.

Still.

Her throat suddenly tightened and her eyes burned. She slowly brushed back the lock of hair that had fallen over his forehead. She ran her knuckles down his cheek. Leaned over and gently pressed her mouth to his, softly rubbing until he made a low growl and caught her head in his hands, deepening the kiss. She pulled back, feeling as if her nerves were ready to pop out from beneath her skin. She looped her fingers through his, and straightened again, pulling.

He rose and she silently led him out of the blinding bright kitchen into the dark hall to her bedroom at the end of the hall.

She hadn't closed the blinds entirely and

the moonlight outside shined through them, casting stripes of dim light over her bed.

She didn't stop until her knees brushed the wedding-ring quilt covering the top of it and she turned her back toward him. "It fastens in the back," she told him softly.

His fingers brushed her nape, but he didn't immediately search out the lacings holding the corset tight against her torso. Instead, he fumbled with the clasp holding her hair back.

Waves tumbled free and he ran his fingers through them, slowly spreading the length forward over her shoulders.

Her knees felt weak. She reached back, catching hold of whatever she could reach—his suit coat.

And finally his knuckles brushed against her spine as he worked the lacings loose. He pulled the fine cord completely free, and tossed it aside.

The corset fell forward and she caught it in her hands, pressing it against her breasts as he turned her to face him. "Sit back," he murmured.

Her shaking legs were only too happy to comply. She sat on the side of the bed and sucked in a harsh breath when he tucked his fingertips beneath the lace band at the top of her hose and slowly rolled them down and off her feet.

They landed somewhere near the corset lacing.

Watching her in the dim light, he pulled off his suit coat. Kicked off his shoes and worked loose the buttons on his shirt. Only when he reached for the buckle of his belt did he pause.

Even then, she knew he was giving her a chance to change her mind.

And in that moment, the fear that was almost as great as the desire, slid away.

This was the only man she'd ever wanted to share herself with. And no amount of reasoning seemed able to change that fact.

She slowly lowered the corset and felt her nipples draw up, even more rigid beneath his gaze. The stiff ivory garment fell from her fingertips to the floor and she reached for him, pushing his hands away to unfasten the belt herself. When she'd finished with that, she worked his zipper down, and as if she'd done it a hundred times rather than a handful, she stripped his clothes from him in one smooth stroke.

Her hands grazed over his hard abdomen, up his chest where the smooth skin gave way to the soft crinkle of dark swirls of hair. When she reached his shoulders, she tugged him down. His name was a murmur on her lips.

The stripes of moonlight seemed to undulate over his body as he settled beside her. "I haven't done this in a long while." His voice was gruff. Hushed.

A soft ache spread through her. She slid her thigh over his and leaned over him, her breasts nestling against that warm, hard chest. Everything inside her wept for him.

She pressed her lips against his. "I haven't done this since *you,*" she admitted.

He let out a long, slow breath. His hands glided up her waist. Her spine. Tangled in her hair.

And then all semblance of patience snapped. He dragged her beneath him, his mouth on hers. His hands raced over her. Tempting. Taunting. Finding.

And when she couldn't stand another second of waiting, couldn't stand another moment of his tormenting, seductive touch without *more*, he knew it, and settled against her, filling her, for she was as impatient as he. And when she heard him groan her name, when she felt herself splintering apart, he swallowed the sobs that she couldn't hold back.

And she knew that once again she'd never be the same.

Chapter 11

After, with Max's arm thrown over her shoulders, holding her snugly against him, Sarah slept.

Deeply. Soundly.

Not even the strident ringing of her telephone penetrated at first. Maybe it wouldn't have at all, if Max hadn't muttered something under his breath and pulled that warm, heavy, wonderfully shaped arm away from her.

She managed to pry open her eyes a fraction.

Sunlight had replaced the bars of soft moonlight.

Her wedding-ring quilt was tangled around their legs. They were sharing one pillow—the other two had ended up on the floor somewhere along the way. She could see them resting carelessly on the floor near the doorway.

"Phone's ringing." His voice was rusty with sleep.

"Why?" She closed her eyes again, turning toward him as he rolled onto his back and instinctively fitted herself against his side.

His hand dropped onto her shoulder, his fingers lazily tracing circles over it. "You'd have to answer it to know that."

"Mmm." Her foot slid over his shin. Her knee brushed his hair-roughened thigh. So many textures. So many sensations.

He gave a rough chuckle and tumbled her onto her back as he rolled over, lifting his head, looking around the bedroom. "Where's your phone?"

It was still ringing. "In the kitchen."

"Why isn't it in here?"

She slid her hands around his waist as he climbed over her. "Because I don't want it waking me *up*," she said pointedly. "Let it ring. The machine will pick up."

He dropped a kiss on her forehead, and kept moving, right off the bed.

She shivered and dragged the quilt more closely around her as he walked, naked and bold as brass, out of her bedroom and down the hall. A second later, she heard him answer the phone. "It's 7 a.m.," he greeted the caller. "It better be important."

She pressed her head into the pillow, cringing. Sensibility was slow in coming, but she knew that a man answering her phone was definitely going to cause some talk.

She heard his footsteps padding back along the hall and stop when he reached the bedroom.

"If that's my mother or father," she mumbled from the pillow she'd pressed to her face, "we are *both* in big trouble."

He didn't answer and she lowered the pillow.

His dark brows were pulled down low over his brow. He ought to have not looked as fierce as he did considering he was standing there as naked as the day he was born, albeit far more grown than an innocent babe. And even though now was not the time—judging from his black expression—to be wallowing breathlessly in the sheer, masculine beauty of him, she couldn't help it.

"It's not your parents," he said flatly.

She moistened her lips. "Who—"

"Your knight-errant."

"What?"

"Brody Paine." He grabbed his pants and started pulling them on.

"He's probably calling about schoolwork for Megan," she said hurriedly.

His lips twisted. "Most people consider this a holiday weekend and the sun's barely up."

"You've got no reason to sound suspicious." She shoved back her heavy hair and slid off the bed, snatching up the first thing her hand came in contact with, which happened to be her corset.

His gaze followed her movements, fastening on the garment in her hands. "Sure about that?"

Her lips tightened and she dropped the corset, grabbing his white shirt, instead. She pulled it around her shoulders, clutching it together at her waist and sailed past him.

Worry was tightening her stomach, which didn't make keeping up the front against him any easier. She hurried into the kitchen and snatched up the receiver where it was resting on the table. "Brody? This is Sarah."

"He standing there listening?"

She didn't have to glance over her shoulder to know that Max was standing in the doorway because she could practically feel his gaze boring a hole between her shoulder blades. "Sure," she answered brightly.

"We got a problem."

Her stomach tightened even more. "Oh?"

"Roberta—the agent who spelled me last night—has got some fricking bug. She's been puking all morning. I've got something I need to see to. Megan needs someone to stay with her."

"I—well, I suppose I could. For how long?"

"Just today. I should be back tonight. If I'm not, we'll get more backup here by then."

"Could Megan come here?"

He sighed, sounding completely frustrated. "That's not exactly protocol."

As far as Sarah had ever been able to determine, there really wasn't a strict protocol about much of anything where Hollins-Winword was concerned. What the agency's concern was, was safety. Personal safety. Corporate safety. National and international safety. She was just a very small cog in one small facet. "It'll be fine," she assured, even though she really wasn't confident of any such thing.

She *was* concerned that Megan might slip on the cover story if they ran into anyone in town—and given the explosion of relatives around because of the holiday and the wedding, it was likely that Sarah would be encountering someone. And she was definitely concerned that Max was already suspicious where Brody was concerned.

It was ridiculous, of course.

The man had no reason to be suspicious.

Except that Brody Paine isn't who you've said he is, and your involvement with him isn't coincidental at all.

She swatted away the irksome truth.

Max had been used to a certain level of excitement when it came to his work. Weaver couldn't possibly come close to the challenges that had been presented to him in Los Angeles. He was looking for shadows that weren't there.

She heard Brody curse under his breath. "Fine. She can stay there. But keep it to yourself."

"Yeah. That'll work," she said dryly. She was supposed to be driving around to pick up donations for the upcoming holiday boutique. "Bring her when you're ready." She hung up the phone and turned to face Max.

He'd pulled on his trousers, but hadn't fastened the button, and they hung low on his hips, exposing the fine line of hair arrowing downward from his navel. His arms were crossed over his bare chest, and his biceps bulged.

It was distracting just to look at the man. He might joke about feeling old, but in her opinion, he looked hard, fit and impossibly perfect. "I'm going to mind Megan Paine for the rest of the day," she told him. "Her dad's in a bind."

"So he calls you."

"I'm probably one of the few people he knows around here, because of Megan's schoolwork," she dismissed. "Want coffee?" She headed toward the coffeemaker sitting on the counter next to the stove.

What Max wanted was an answer to the reason she kept avoiding his eyes. And he wanted to keep her away from Brody Paine. Not only because he'd seen the way the guy looked at Sarah, but because the man was a complete unknown. Despite Max's efforts to learn something—anything—about him, Brody Paine remained totally off the grid.

Given the timing of his arrival in town and the reason for Max even being there in the first place, it was a coincidence he didn't like.

Brody Paine could *easily* be connected even though Max had yet to find proof.

"I don't like him," he told her.

She laughed slightly as she filled the coffee filter. "Brody? For pity's sake, Max, I've told you. There's nothing between us."

"Keep it that way."

She pushed the filter in place and jabbed the power button with a little too much enthusiasm. Her eyes were the color of a frozen-over lake when they turned his way. "Excuse me?"

He dropped his arms and moved next to her at the counter. She was no longer clutching his shirt together between her breasts and it had fallen open, revealing a wedge of smooth, satiny skin that had the blood warming in his veins. "There's something wrong where that guy is concerned and I want you to stay away from him."

She shoved the canister holding the coffee grounds back against the others that matched it. "Are you that bored with Weaver already that you're conjuring up drug dealers and murderers? Or are you just afraid that he might try to get me into bed?"

"He'd be a damn fool not to try that. And, as it happens, there's nothing all that boring about Weaver."

She looked disbelieving. "You're telling me you're satisfied stopping a speeder now and then and writing up reports for fender benders in the shopping center's parking lot? Please. You thrived on the hunt, Max. I might have been naive about everything else when I ran into you in California at Frowley-Hughes, but even I recognized *that*. Before we know it, you'll be heading on, looking for something a *lot* more interesting than what Weaver's got to offer."

Getting into an argument wasn't going to solve anything, particularly when she was right about one thing—he *did* have plans to move on. Plans that, by the day, were becoming annoyingly murky. "Trust me on this, Sarah. I'm asking you. Please. Stay away from him."

Her lashes lowered. The high color in her cheeks slowly retreated. "I've already agreed to watch Megan for him. What's one afternoon? She's a sweet little girl who's lost everything that mattered to her."

"Except dear ol' dad."

"Except Brody," she agreed. The coffeemaker hissed softly between them. "I wouldn't turn my back on Eli," she pointed out after a moment. "I won't do that with Megan, either."

"What's he got to do that's so important he can't take care of his kid?"

"I have no idea." She pulled down two white mugs from the cupboard above her head and rested her palms over the tops of them, giving him a look. "You've left Eli alone with your mother and you've been here all night since we…since we—"

He circled her narrow wrist with his fingers and lifted her hand. Her fingers curled downward and he pressed his index finger over her pulse, feeling the beat. "That's different. I let my mom know where I was."

"You don't know that it's different. You're just assuming that Brody doesn't have a perfectly valid reason for needing someone to watch Megan."

"Your pulse is racing."

She moistened her lips, looking wry and pained at the same time. "Pardon me. I'm not so used to having a half-naked man in my kitchen."

He lifted her wrist until it was above her head and slowly revolved her until she was facing him, her back pressed against the counter top. Her other arm was free and the sleeve of his too-large shirt was falling loosely off her shoulder. "You meant it then. That there hasn't been anyone."

She bent that arm, crossing it over her chest and halting the descent of his shirt. "Did *you* mean it?"

That he hadn't been with a woman since Jennifer? Admitting it in the cold light of morning was a far sight more difficult than it had been in the dark, drugging warmth of Sarah's inviting bed. "Yeah."

Her lips softened and the icy-lake blue

thawed. "I'm sorry you and Eli had to go through losing her. Nobody should have to lose anyone to cancer."

"She knew about you. She felt badly about everything. Told me that I needed to get in touch with you."

She was silent, absorbing that. The long line of her lovely throat worked. "But you didn't."

"I couldn't," he corrected. He closed his fingers around the bottom of his shirt that she was pretending to wear and slowly pulled on it. It began sliding downward between her bent arm and her breast. "Walking away once was all I could manage."

Her eyes hadn't merely thawed. They glimmered. Sheer. Wet. "Don't tell me things you don't mean, Max. I can take nearly anything but that."

"I mean every word." He continued pulling the bottom of the shirt. Beneath her arm, the swell of her breast was revealed. He kept up the pressure, slowly and inexorably drawing the shirt aside, until her nipple, tight and raspberry sweet, peeked free above her forearm. "Now you. Did you mean it?"

The coffeepot behind her gurgled and sighed its last drops of brew.

Her gaze lifted to his. "The men I've occasionally dated—I, we haven't—" She broke off, her cheeks flushing. "There's only been you," she finished huskily.

It humbled him, he realized, hearing her confirm it.

He slid his arm beneath the shirt, circling her waist, fingers spreading over the gentle flare of hip. He lifted her and she gasped as he settled her on the counter's edge.

He dropped his head, finding that taunting nipple with his lips and dragged the shirt from her, tossing it away.

She let out a shuddering sigh, her fingers flexing, kneading against his shoulders. His hands slid along her smooth thighs, slipping between, nudging them apart, making room for himself.

"Max, oh *God*—we're in my kitchen!"

"And I'm starving," he said against her.

The skin of her inner thighs was the smoothest thing he'd ever felt in his life.

The down at the apex the softest.

The flesh the sweetest.

She jerked when he touched her there. Tasted her there. Her hands scrambled against the flat countertop, finding no purchase, and knocked into his shoulders, and finally settled into his hair, holding him to her. She moaned, shuddering. Quivering. And finally, too quickly, too slowly—convulsing.

He looked up at her. Her lips, soft and rosy, parted as she dragged in long breaths. Her eyes still had tears in them, but they seemed to gleam with a deep blue flame. Her reddish-blond hair licked down her back and he could actually see her heart beating through her pale, delicate skin.

Her gaze tangled with his, and watching her, never breaking that contact, he kissed the flat belly and felt it spasm beneath his lips. He kissed the valley between her breasts and felt her heartbeat pound against him.

And when he reached her lips, they were moving, chanting his name again and again.

He would never get enough of this woman.

He pulled her off the counter and her legs came around his hips and he turned to go to the bedroom.

It was Saturday, he reasoned with the few remaining reasonable cells functioning in his brain.

His son was taken care of by his grandmother. He wasn't on deputy duty because Tommy Potter had offered to take the shift. The guy was always wanting extra shifts. This time Max had taken him up on it and he was glad.

He could spend the entire day making love to—

"The doorbell's ringing," Sarah muttered against his mouth. "Oh, good grief, they're already here!" She was suddenly pushing against Max, swinging her legs free.

He either had to let her go, or they'd both end up in a tangle on the hall floor. All he caught was a glimpse of her shapely, nude derriere as she scrambled, practically on all fours, into her bedroom at the end of the short hall.

The door slammed shut.

Leaving him standing there, hard, and alone.

"Dammit." He could have said a lot worse as he saw Brody Paine peering around the side of the window next to the door, trying to see through the curtains hanging there. Thank God, Max knew it was a lot harder to see *into* the house, than it was to see out of it.

He strode into the kitchen and swiped up his shirt, yanking it over his shoulders and fastening the bottom few buttons. Then he grabbed open the door, and glared at the man standing on the porch.

Brody's gaze went over Max's state of undress. "Sarah here?" His voice was mild, but he did sort of step in front of the skinny girl hovering behind him.

Max turned away. Annoyed, horny, suspicious, and quite possibly jealous didn't make for a welcoming demeanor. "Sarah," he barked.

"I'm here, I'm here." She was skidding back into the room on stocking feet, having thrown on a deep blue sweat suit that looked like it was made for lounging on the cover of a fashion magazine rather than for working up an actual sweat.

She was dragging her hair back into a ponytail holder and if there was any sign of the woman who'd just come apart in his hands on her kitchen counter, he'd be damned if he could see it.

Avoiding his eyes, she hurried past him to the door and pushed the storm door wide. "Hi, Megan. Brody. Come on in."

Max stomped down the hall to the bedroom and slammed the door behind him.

Yeah, he was acting about as mature as Eli, but at the moment, he didn't give a flying flip.

He pulled on his shoes and socks. Sarah was obviously going to be busy watching over the girl.

And Max—like it or not—had a job to do.

Brody was heading *somewhere* that day.

Max was going to find out exactly where.

And then, maybe, he could close the file on Weaver.

For some reason, that possibility was losing its appeal.

He pushed off the tumbled bed and slowly picked up the pillows that had fallen to the floor. He pressed one to his face.

It smelled of Sarah.

He set both pillows on the bed and left the room.

Sarah and Brody were facing each other, the full distance of the living room between them.

Megan was hovering behind her father, misery practically screaming from her narrow shoulders, clad in a knitted sweater that looked about a full size too large. Her dishwater blond hair hung lank alongside her solemn face and her too-big brown eyes followed every movement Max made.

He picked up his coat that he didn't even remember leaving on the couch. He eyed Sarah for a moment. "Remember the locks."

She nibbled her lip. Nodded.

Ignoring Brody altogether, Max left, going out through the back door.

Who the hell was he kidding?

He knew why closing the case and getting

out of Weaver didn't fill him with joy any longer.

And she was inside that tiny house, lying her sweet tush off to him about what she was doing.

Chapter 12

"Come on, Megan. Why don't you try on this one?" Sarah held up the vividly colored blouse she'd plucked off the rack.

They were in Classic Charms, Sarah's favorite shop on Main Street. It had been there for less than a year, but even in that time had gained a rapid popularity, carrying an eclectic mix of clothing, furniture, and various bric-a-brac.

On the weekend following Thanksgiving, it was doing a pretty brisk business, too, and Sarah had been about at her wit's end thinking of something to entertain Megan.

They'd already driven around collecting the items for the school boutique, which was probably more than Brody would have approved of. Driving over to the mall in Braden would have undoubtedly sent him over the edge when she'd have to tell him, and the shopping center on the other side of town held little appeal to Sarah.

But browsing down Main? When she'd proposed the idea to Megan, the girl had agreed, almost as if she'd believed she had no choice. Probably because everything that had happened in her young life lately had definitely *not* been her choice.

The girl was so excruciatingly sad it was heartbreaking.

"What do you think?" Sarah waggled the padded hanger and the purple-and-blue tie-dyed fabric seemed to shimmer a little. "It'd look great with your coloring."

Megan's lashes barely lifted long enough for her to look at the blouse. She'd hardly spoken five sentences all morning.

Not that she was rude. Inordinately polite, if anything. "I'm sorry, Miss Clay. But I don't have money."

Sarah tossed the blouse over her arm and crouched down in front of Megan. "Well, I do," she countered gently. "And I *love* to shop, but my closet is chock-full already. This is a gift from me. So all you have to decide is if you like the colors." She looked at the clothing rack—which was actually an old-fashioned phone booth with pipes sticking out of it at all sorts of odd angles. "Or do you prefer something else?"

Megan's fingers lightly touched the fabric, as if she couldn't quite resist. She finally leaned forward a little and lowered her voice. "Mr. Brody doesn't take me out shopping," she said, almost inaudibly.

"I'm not Mr. Brody," Sarah whispered back. She squeezed Megan's thin shoulder.

If Sarah accomplished anything that day, she was going to get a smile out of this girl.

And, it kept her mind off the fact that when Max had left her house that morning, he'd said nothing whatsoever about calling her. Or seeing her.

She, of course, hadn't wanted to make an issue about it in front of Brody, and had cowardly said absolutely nothing.

She'd just watched Max walk out her door.

It had been a dismaying moment of déjà vu.

"Well? Want to try it on? Tara has a dressing room behind the counter there. I'll wait right outside the curtain," she promised.

The girl nibbled her lip again. Then shyly nodded.

Triumphant, Sarah straightened. She took

Megan's hand and they walked to the back of the shop. She handed over the top to Megan and pulled back the long curtain that afforded complete privacy for the single changing room. "You have to show me," she told Megan. "When you have it on. No switching back to your sweater before I get to see."

Megan ducked her chin. She nodded and pulled the curtain down.

Sarah hummed under her breath along with the Christmas carols that were playing on the shop's sound system. Maybe she'd take Megan out to the *C*. The girl might like a horse ride as much as Eli had.

In fact, maybe Eli would like another lesson and she could kill two birds with one stone.

The expression made her mentally wince given how Megan's parents had died.

Was it any wonder the child was skittish? She was an exceptionally smart girl. She knew the sort of danger she'd been in before they'd brought her to Weaver.

Sighing a little, Sarah toyed with the pens that were stored in a milk-glass vase next to the vintage cash register and whirled back around when she heard Megan whisper her name.

"Oh, Megan. Look at you! That is *so* pretty. Do you like it?"

Megan looked at herself in the tall mirror that lined one side of the dressing room. She nodded before casting a worried look at Sarah. "Can I try on some others?"

"Honey, you can try on everything here right down to lampshades on your head if you like."

Megan's lips lifted just a hair. She walked back to the rack of clothes and studied them carefully.

Tara Browning, the shop owner, walked behind the cash register and smiled at Sarah. "Getting a start on Christmas shopping?"

"I suppose I should be," she admitted.

Would Max still be in Weaver by then? Christmas was four weeks away.

Turning off the thought proved difficult, so Sarah joined Megan at the rack. Only every garment that she pulled out and held up to her own chest had her wondering how Max would like it.

She stopped looking, and sat down experimentally on the wide, nubby couch that, according to the hand-lettered signs, could be ordered in three-dozen other fabrics. She was watching the glass door that opened out onto Main Street, and smiled when she saw Eli come into view, followed closely by Genna Scalise.

The woman definitely had the whole crutch thing down.

Sarah rose and crossed the shop. "I was just thinking about you," she said to Eli.

Genna pulled her long knitted scarf off her head and unbuttoned her coat. "Seems to be going around," she replied. "Eli's talked nonstop about you and the day we had at your family's place. I still can't tell you how much we enjoyed it."

"We were all glad to have you," Sarah assured. From the corner of her eye, she watched Megan go into the changing room again. "So, is the Christmas shopping season calling to you, too?"

Genna nodded. "Have a few gifts to pick up. Don't know *what* to get my son. Ever since Tony, he's had it in his head that he should only get *me* gifts, doesn't want to take any in return." She finished working out of her coat, and Sarah took it from her, laying it over the back of a bar stool that was doing double duty as a plant stand. "I've also been hearing nothing but talk around town today about Leandra and Evan's wedding yesterday. I was sorry to miss it. Have they left for a honeymoon?"

"Last night. Five days in balmy Mexico."

Genna's eyes twinkled. "Sounds lovely.

Max and Jennifer went to Mexico after they were married."

Sarah waited for the pang, but when it came, it was not as sharp as it once would have been. "It's a popular place. I'd better check on Megan's progress. Oh." She turned back to Genna. "If Eli's interested, I thought he might like to go riding again today. I'm going to take Megan, too. They might enjoy meeting each other and I *know* they'll both enjoy the horses. I'm thinking maybe around two or three?"

"I can't seem to place her," Genna said, looking beyond Sarah to the girl.

"She and her dad are staying out at the Holley place. Haven't been in town too long."

"Oh, of course. He's the writer." Seeming satisfied she'd placed them, she looked at Sarah again. "I'm sure Eli would love to go with you. Particularly since Max is out of town for a few days. But I'm sure he told *you* that." She looked pleased at the idea.

Sarah tucked her tongue between her teeth for a moment, feeling her face flush. Naturally Genna knew that Max hadn't come home last night. But Sarah *hadn't* known that Max had left town. "Right," she baldly lied.

Genna was already crossing the shop, heading for a display of delicate Christmas ornaments. "I don't know what case he's working on, but he's sure putting in some ridiculous hours." She picked up a translucent green bulb. "Pretty, isn't it?"

"Yes." But Sarah wasn't really looking at the ornament. She was too busy telling herself that Max's abrupt disappearance was nothing to worry about.

She'd hear from him.

She would.

The self-assurance was definitely wearing thin by midweek. By the *end* of the week, it was bare threads. Only the fact that Eli was still coming to class every day—and primarily behaving himself—assured her that Max hadn't just gone from Weaver for good.

So, when he suddenly appeared the morning of the holiday boutique being held in the auditorium at her school, acting as if nothing was amiss, she told herself her irritation was justified.

"Where do you want the rolls, Sarah?" Justine Leoni drew back Sarah's attention from Max's unexpected entrance. She was carrying an enormous, flat bakery box that smelled delicious. She had three more boxes stacked on a rolling cart behind her.

Ignore Max. Sarah gestured to the tables

to one side of the auditorium. "All the food'll be over there. Need some help?"

Justine waved off the offer, and deftly maneuvered the cart, even with her full hands.

Sarah's gaze started straying toward the doorway and Max once again.

More irritated with herself than anyone, including him, she snatched up one of the fresh wreaths that she hadn't finished hanging around the room, and headed for the ladder where she'd left it, directly opposite the doorway. She looped the wreath over her arm and started up the rungs. The soothing fragrance of the fresh balsam surrounded her.

"Looks like somebody shook up a bottle of fizzy Christmas soda and let it explode in here," Max said, below her.

She kept her eye on the light fixture from which she was hanging the wreath. "Hello to you, too." She twisted the floral wire on the back of the wreath together and looped it over the light.

The wreath settled neatly against the wall and she adjusted the bright red bow at the bottom of it.

"Eli told me he put my name on a list last week to help out at this shindig."

She'd passed out the sign-up sheet on Monday. "Don't worry, Max." She descended the ladder, her gaze skimming over him. He wore jeans and a leather bomber jacket and aside from smelling dismayingly good, she thought he looked tired. "Plenty of other parents are coming to help."

He slanted a look at her. "Meaning what?"

She reached the floor. "Meaning you don't have to feel obligated." The ladder folded together with a loud snap and she tilted it against her shoulder to drag it over to the last light fixture.

He grabbed the ladder, and would have lifted it right out from her hands if she hadn't held on. "Who says anything about obligation? Maybe I want to be here."

She recognized that fighting over the ladder would be silly so she let go of it. "Right."

"Where's this coming from?"

"You're clearly a busy man." Her voice was dulcet.

"Yes, I am. Yet I have the distinct feeling that those words aren't a satisfactory excuse. You're angry."

She picked up the last wreath. "Put the ladder there, if you're so determined to help."

He set the ladder in place. Spread the legs of it. "Sarah—"

She could feel her eyes burning and felt like she was all of sixteen years old, and had been jilted for a school dance. Either she was an adult, or she wasn't.

She set the wreath over a ladder rung and looked at him. "Why didn't you tell me you were leaving town?"

"It was work stuff."

Her lips twisted. "Yes. I believe I *heard* that. It would have been nice to hear it from you. But, you know, it was a necessary reminder for me."

His lips were tight. "About what?"

"Not to get used to you being around."

He stifled an oath. "I'm not going anywhere."

She lifted her eyebrows. "Really? That's not what Eli thinks. He specifically shared with me how you've told him you're only here until your mother is healed up. He told me and I still—" She broke off, realizing her voice was rising. She picked up the wreath again. "I still slept with you," she said for his ears only. "My mistake."

He grabbed the sides of the ladder as she started up it. "This is *not* seven years ago, Sarah. Nothing is the same as it was then."

She rapidly stuck the wreath in place and quickly descended the ladder once more. He was right about that. The feelings she had for him now seemed frighteningly new. "Only thing that has changed is geography," she lied.

"That and the propensity you've acquired for keeping secrets."

Her lips parted. "*Secrets?*" She darted a look around them, hoping they weren't drawing more attention. She still had to live in Weaver once he went on his way. "Compared to you, my life is an open book!"

"Really." He jerked his chin, his gaze moving past her. "Then what the hell are you doing with him?"

She turned to see what he was looking at and wanted to groan out loud at the sight of Brody Paine.

Of all times for him to take her up on her regular invitations to include Megan in at least one of the school functions. "Get your mind out of the gutter," she told Max stiffly, and crossed the room to greet Megan.

The girl was wearing the colorful tie-dyed blouse and looked even happier than she had the afternoon that Sarah had taken her and Eli riding. "I like the shirt, Meggie."

The girl's cheeks colored, seeming pleased. "Thank you." She tugged on Brody's arm. "Can I go see Eli… Dad?" She managed to tack on that last.

Brody nodded. His eyes tracked the child's

progress as she crossed the room to where Eli was hanging over a chair, watching Dee Crowder set up the Pin the Beard on the Santa game.

"So, Brody. What spurred this nice surprise?"

Brody pushed his hands in the pockets of his jeans. If Sarah weren't so entirely consumed with a certain black-haired deputy, she might be more inclined to appreciate the view he presented.

Brody Paine *was* a good-looking man. And judging by the arch looks Dee was sending toward Sarah, that fact was definitely being noticed.

"They're pulling me from this gig," he murmured. "About one more week."

Dismay filled her. "Already? But—but what happens with Megan?"

He lifted his shoulder. "The guy who did her parents is finally taken care of. And you know the drill. Everyone moves on—no more contact."

She did know the drill. She just had never particularly liked it. Now, with Megan, she liked it even less. She wasn't ready to see the girl disappear from their lives. "Can't you at least stay with her through the holidays?

For heaven's sake, she deserves a little consistency."

"I don't call those shots, Sarah." A hint of sympathy crossed his face. "And you're not supposed to get so involved that you lose your objectivity, either."

She huffed, crossing her arms and looking away. If she'd been objective, she never would have agreed to be part of Hollins-Winword in the first place.

Across the room, Dee had now enlisted Megan and Eli. They were helping her pin up the big Santa posters and both the children seemed to be having a grand time from the looks of it. "I want to talk to Coleman Black," Sarah said abruptly.

Brody's expression changed. "So would a lot of people, doll. Doesn't mean it'll happen."

She gave him a hard look.

He made a face. "Ask your uncle. Get better luck through him than me."

"My *uncle?*"

"Tristan. He's—well *hell*." His expression was almost comical with surprise. "You don't know, do you?"

She'd never liked feeling in the dark. "Know what?" she asked warily.

"Tell *him* who you want to see," Brody said simply. Then he lifted his arms as if to end that particular topic. "So, I'm here. Not gonna drag Megan away now. Even I'm not that callous. Where do you want me to work?" He looked around. "I assume you *do* want me to work."

She exhaled, feeling completely off-kilter. Her uncle Tristan designed video games. What could he possibly have to do with Hollins-Winword? "I need someone to sell raffle tickets," she said.

He looked disgusted. But, when she plunked an enormous roll of tickets in his hands, he didn't decline.

Then she turned and faced Max.

Just one more man to deal with, she told herself.

Only Max wasn't just anything, and no matter how many times she tried to tell herself that, she couldn't make herself buy it.

He was leaning against the side of a long table, openly watching her exchange with Brody, and as she headed toward him, she couldn't help noticing again how tired he looked. There were dark circles beneath his changeable eyes, and the lines fanning out from the corners seemed deeper than usual.

"He's volunteering," she told him evenly.

"I thought only school parents were doing that."

"Maybe he *is* a school parent. You don't know everything that's gone on this past week."

"Megan would be in Eli's class and Eli didn't say squat about her, other than to talk about how you took them both riding at your folks' place. As you told me once, you *are* the only third-grade teacher here."

"You can do trash duty."

Unfortunately, the terse assignment only seemed to amuse him. His lips stretched. "Yes, ma'am. I'm here to serve."

Her teeth clamped together and she turned away, heading toward a cluster of parents who'd arrived and were waiting for direction.

Fortunately, Sarah didn't have much time to worry about Max after that. Not when there was a line of people waiting at the door the moment they officially opened their auditorium-sized boutique. Things didn't start to settle down until just before they were ready to close their doors at the end of the day, and Sarah had a chance to sit down and man a table herself.

It was the first break she'd had all day.

Within minutes, Max was emptying a trash can behind her table, whistling tunelessly along with the Christmas carols being played on the school's sound system, and Brody was sitting down beside her. He plopped a big paper bag on the floor between them. It was filled nearly to overflowing with the ticket halves from which the drawings would be taken at the end of the day. "Sold 'em all," he announced.

"Maybe you missed your calling," she murmured, amazed.

"Speaking of which," Max said, his voice annoyingly smooth, "what is it that you write?"

Sarah rested her elbows on the table and pressed her hands to her cheeks. She was tired enough to let the two men battle whatever pissing contest they had going on between them.

"Technical reports," Brody said easily. "Nothing anybody ever remembers me for, I'm afraid, but it pays the bills."

She made herself smile when Tommy Potter ambled over to the table and started picking through the arrangement of homemade wrapping paper and gift tags. "How're you doing, Tommy?"

The deputy shrugged. "Fair enough." He picked up a plastic baggie filled with gold tags on which Sarah herself had calligraphed the greetings. "Max, you want to trade shifts again tomorrow? I could use the extra time in the old paycheck this month."

"Sorry. Can't." Max whipped a fresh bag inside the barrel. "Try Dave." Dave Ruiz was the third deputy, Sarah knew, though he spent more time in the Braden office than in Weaver.

"No problem. Will do." Tommy flipped open his wallet and handed over some bills. "Thanks, Sarah. Nice turnout you're having here. Good job."

She gave him his change. "Thanks. Stop and visit Dee on your way out, why don't you?"

He seemed to flush a little, and ducked his chin, mumbling something inaudible before ambling away again.

"Only time that guy mumbles is when it comes to a pretty woman," Max murmured. "Can't shut the guy up when we're at the station house."

"He's shy," Sarah excused.

"And I think we'll be outta here." Brody leaned back in the metal folding chair to stretch. "Gotta feed Megan something other than peanut brittle and Christmas cookies."

"Brody—bring her to the holiday pageant at least. It's just next week. Thursday evening."

His smile was sympathetic, but noncommittal. "We'll see."

She hadn't liked that phrase as a girl and nothing had changed since.

The moment Brody vacated the seat beside her, Max assumed it. His arm brushed against hers as he folded his hands on top of the nearly empty table.

She shifted, putting a few more inches between them. Across the room, Brody had collected Megan and the girl turned, sending a wave in her direction.

Sarah's heart squeezed. She lifted her hand.

"What's wrong? You look like you're never going to see her again."

She dropped her hand, her cheeks heating. "Not at all. She's a nice girl. She's lost a lot in her life. You know what it's like for a child to lose a parent."

"She looks a damn sight more animated than she did last week," he admitted. "Think Eli's got a crush on her or something the way he jabbers on about her." He idly picked up the last of the baggies filled with tags. "He's no writer."

"You're like a dog with a bone."

"Been compared to worse things. What do you want to bet me that you know what he *is?*"

She snatched up the bag of raffle tickets. "Time for the drawing."

He stretched out one leg, settling deeper into the folding chair. "I'm not going anywhere."

"Yet." She didn't wait for his reaction as she headed to the small stage and the microphone there. "All right, ladies and gents, time for the big moment. I need someone up here for a little help, though."

A bunch of hands flew up in the air, mostly belonging to students of the school. She pointed out several whom she knew to be first-graders and they all raced up to her, jockeying for position. She held the bag where they could reach in. "Dig deep now, and pull out just one ticket."

Fierce expressions of concentration crossed their young faces as one by one they drew and Sarah read off the numbers for the prizes—everything from free meals and massages to a cord of chopped firewood to a weekend trip to Las Vegas. The last prize—considered by some to be the granddaddy of them all—was a year's worth of Sunday breakfasts at Ruby's.

Sarah joggled the bag, smiling over the catcalls to mix the tickets even more, and took the ticket that emerged courtesy of the last young ticket-puller. She held it up and read off the numbers, watching the crowd. And when

Max rose and began making his way forward, she managed to keep her smile in place. He worked through the back-slapping congratulations and came up beside her on the stage where she held the envelope holding the certificate Justine had generously donated.

Sarah flicked off the microphone. "I'm sure Justine won't mind if you give the prize to your mother," she murmured as she handed over the envelope.

His fingers brushed hers. "Why would I do that?"

"A year's a long time." She picked up the bag and held it against her chest, turning to flip on the microphone and thank everyone for their support.

When she was finished, Max followed her off the little stage. "A year's not so long, depending on who you spend it with."

She swallowed, her heart giving an odd lurch. "Eli *does* make time fly. Excuse me. I have to collect all the money now." She turned and practically raced away from him.

But she knew she was really racing away from the longing to believe he actually meant her.

Chapter 13

After the school event, Sarah dropped the money they'd collected in the night depository at the bank and headed home.

But she couldn't relax. Not after Max's presence all that day. Not after what he'd said.

But he hadn't suggested seeing her that evening, hadn't done anything but collect Eli and head out after he'd hauled bag after bag of trash to the containers behind the school building.

She made a few phone calls. Leandra, who was back from her honeymoon with Evan and so distracted that Sarah was half-afraid of just what she'd interrupted with her phone call. Her cousin, Lucy, who had a flight out to

New York the following morning. She even tried her uncle Tristan's number, only Justin—their youngest—told her that his folks had gone out of town for the day.

When she found herself dialing Genna Scalise's number, she quickly hung up the phone. Chasing after Max was something she would *not* do. Not again. No amount of explaining the past could change her feelings on that score.

But as she was pulling out the box of Christmas decorations in preparation for decorating her *own* place, her gaze kept falling on the recent purchases she'd made at Classic Charms. She'd gone back to the shop and had picked up every single item that Megan had seemed to like. They were already wrapped in festive Christmas packages.

Only Megan would be gone before Christmas.

For all Sarah knew, Max could well be gone by then, too, no matter *how* many free breakfasts he'd won at Ruby's.

Knowing that Max was at the root of her restlessness didn't stop Sarah from doing at least one concrete, productive thing.

She gathered up Megan's gifts and loaded them in the front seat of her car. The late hour didn't prevent her from driving out to the Holley place. She knew Brody and Megan would be there. She just didn't know for how many more *days* they'd be there.

The graded road out to the old farmhouse was passable. It had been snowplowed, but time and use had worn deep ruts that she wasn't entirely successful in avoiding. So she bumped along the miles and was particularly grateful when the single light burning on the front porch came into sight.

Though it was nearing ten o'clock when she arrived, she hadn't even doused her headlights before several more lights around the house flashed on, startling her for a moment.

Security lights, she realized. Probably motionautomated.

She parked her car and gathered up the items she'd brought for Megan and headed toward the porch.

Well into the darkness, Max watched the front door of the farmhouse open even before Sarah could knock. Brody Paine looked out, casting a quick look around, then practically pulled Sarah inside.

The door closed.

"What the hell is my niece doing here?" Beside Max, Sawyer's mild voice was belied by the tension suddenly emanating from him.

Max knew how the man felt. "Good question." They'd had the Holley place under surveillance for more than a week, ever since an unusual money flow had been traced to Paine, the timing of which coincided too neatly with a major drug ring bust that had been made in Arizona that week. Then, another package of meth had been discovered just that morning on a trailer belonging to Jefferson Clay.

There'd been no unusual activity around the property though, until that afternoon, when a stranger had arrived in a Hummer bearing a false registration. He'd left after less than an hour, and the tail Max had assigned to the vehicle reported that it was left in the parking lot of the Cheyenne airport. Unfortunately, the driver of the Hummer had been lost inside the airport.

Unfathomable to Max, but stuff happened.

"I prefer good answers," Sawyer countered. Max knew the sheriff wasn't entirely convinced of Brody's involvement. "What was she carrying?"

"Looked like Christmas presents to me," Max murmured, knowing perfectly well that the other man had seen the same gift-wrapped boxes. "Maybe they're for Megan. Sarah seems attached to the kid. But I know one thing—" he pushed open the door of the vehicle "—I'm going to find out." He checked his weapon, and yanked his coat on, shoving his radio in the side pocket.

"No warrant, yet," Sawyer reminded. "This may be your show, son, but I wouldn't want anyone slipping through legal technicalities."

Max didn't either. "I'm just a jealous boyfriend," he assured smoothly, and started toward the house. Unfortunately, the explanation was more true than not.

He heard Sawyer swear under his breath and the man who eschewed guns slowly reached for the rifle hanging in the rack behind his head.

Max didn't particularly like guns, either. Hell, if the truth be known, he was pretty sick to death of them.

Beneath his boots, the gravel—half muddy, half covered with frozen-crisp snow—sounded loud in the still night. He passed Sarah's car, looking in the windows, seeing nothing but a box sitting on the back seat, containing leftovers he recognized from the school sale.

The security lights positioned with military precision around the house were still on. Feeling itchy with exposure, Max rapidly covered the distance to the house, heading up the steps. The door held little resistance to a well-aimed boot, and he almost could hear Sawyer cursing from the vehicle two hundred yards away.

His eyes took in the two figures that turned toward him when the doorjamb splintered. He was hitting the floor, his weapon drawn before Sarah's face could become more than a blur as Brody roughly shoved her aside and trained his own Glock at Max's head.

The other guy was as wide open as Max was—neither had any cover in the sparsely furnished room.

Sarah's startled scream echoed inside his head, but Max didn't take his eyes off Brody. "Put it down," he warned grimly.

"Max." Sarah was scrambling to her feet. "You don't know what you're doing!"

"Stay out of the way—"

"Stay back—"

Both men spoke at the same time.

She ignored both of them. "I won't stay back!" Max wasn't sure if Brody looked more pained than Max felt when she stubbornly stepped right between them.

"Thought you told me he was no threat," Brody said. His voice was cold.

She flapped her arms. "He's not." She glared at Max. "What *are* you doing?"

"My job," he snapped. "Now get out of here. Sawyer's outside. You can explain yourself later."

Her brows rose, nearly disappearing beneath the hair that had tumbled across her forehead. "Explain *myself?*"

Max's weapon didn't waver. He had sweat crawling down his spine, and there'd come a time when he'd probably puke his guts out at the panic he was feeling, seeing Sarah blocking Paine.

"I don't have to explain myself to you, Max Scalise!"

"Oh, fun," Brody drawled, looking suddenly amused. "A lovers' spat."

"Be quiet." Sarah whirled on him. "And put that thing away." She sounded just like Max's first-grade teacher. Only Mrs. Krantz had seemed older than the hills and had scared the bejabbers out of him.

"Him first," Brody said, gesturing with his handgun.

Sarah propped her hands on her hips. "Honestly, Brody, is this how you always do business?"

"It is when some fool crashes through my door in the middle of the friggin' night."

"What business?" The question gritted from between Max's clenched teeth.

A sudden blur of motion launched itself into the room, aiming straight for Sarah.

Max's aim shifted.

"Don't even try," Brody said icily, all semblance of amusement gone. He looked as if he'd just as soon shoot Max as breathe.

Megan was clutching Sarah's legs, mute and clearly terrified. He could see her shaking right through the red flannel nightgown she wore.

Sarah bent over the girl, hugging her and smoothing back the tumbled hair. "It's all right," she soothed. "Nobody's getting hurt." But when she angled a look at Max, her gaze was furious. "There's a perfectly reasonable explanation." She spoke slowly, her gaze taking in both men as if she were speaking to the village idiots.

Brody's expression was stony, and huffing a little, Sarah looked toward Max. "Isn't there?"

Megan hadn't budged her head from Sarah's belly.

"You tell me. Give me a perfectly reasonable explanation why your phone records show you've been in contact with Paine's cell phone since before he even *came* to Weaver."

Her lips parted. "You've been checking my phone records?"

"I've been trying to check *his*," he corrected tightly. Only they'd been extremely difficult to obtain. "What a delightful surprise that, in that process, I kept coming across *your* number."

Her lips looked white. "I… I know Brody professionally, all right? That's all."

"*What* profession?"

"Not the oldest one," she snapped, "So stop giving me a look like I just announced I'm a call girl."

Brody snickered and she shot him a deadly look.

"He's part of an investigation," he said finally.

"*He* is standing right here," Brody inserted blandly.

Sarah ignored him. "Investigation of what?"

"Drug trafficking."

At that, Brody suddenly lowered his weapon and raised his other hand. "Whoa. I think we got a problem here."

"Damn straight." Max didn't trust that casual grip on the Glock. "Put it on the floor and step away."

Sarah looked completely bewildered as Brody slowly complied. He set the gun near Sarah and Megan's feet and backed away.

"That's far enough. Sarah, push the gun over here."

She made a face, but nudged the toe of her brown boot against the weapon. She didn't let go of Megan.

Max snatched up the weapon and unloaded it. He heard the scrape of a shoe and swung his arm around, taking aim at the doorway, but the sight of Sawyer had him lowering his weapon.

"Uncle Sawyer." Sarah sounded painfully relieved. "Thank goodness. We *need* a voice of sanity here."

Whether he regularly carried a weapon or not, Sawyer carried the rifle with ease. "Just a jealous boyfriend?" His voice was dry, giving no real clue to what he really thought.

Max could guess though. Nothing like a royal FUBAR.

"Boyfriend." Sarah sniffed. "Not likely."

"You prefer the word *lover?*" Max drawled.

She flushed and leaned over Megan, whispering to the girl. After a moment, the child unclenched her iron-tight grip and slipped over to Brody.

The man tucked her behind him, and though the motion was protective, it hardly seemed paternal to Max.

Sawyer sighed. "I'm too old for this

crap," he muttered. "Sarah, get the girl there dressed. Seems we need to take a trip to the station house. Get some questions answered."

"With all due respect, Sheriff," Brody said, "you're barking up the wrong tree if you think I'm moving dope."

Sawyer didn't look any more convinced than Max felt. "Sarah," he prompted sharply.

Looking shaken, she ushered the girl out of the room.

"Now." Sawyer looked back at Brody. "Face on the floor. Something tells me you know the position."

Brody snorted and started to laugh, but it died when Max leveled his gun at him. Swearing under his breath, he dropped to the floor, arms and legs spread.

Max knelt over him, taking a little too much joy as he held the man down with his knee to his spine. He frisked the guy, found nothing but a small cell phone in his pocket, and snapped cuffs around his wrists. Then he grabbed Brody's arm and hauled him to his feet.

Sarah, entering the room again with Megan—now dressed in jeans and a sweatshirt instead of that long flannel nightgown—gasped at the sight. "This is all wrong," she said.

"Then we'll get it straightened out," Sawyer said wearily. "Can I trust you to drive yourself and the girl to the station?"

Her shoulders snapped back. She looked insulted. "Of course." Her gaze sent frosty daggers at Max as she picked up her coat from the threadbare couch and pulled it on. But her voice was gentle when she told Megan to get her coat, as well. As soon as the girl pulled it on, Sarah took her hand and they went out the front door.

"All right," Sawyer said. "Let's move it."

Megan was sitting on a molded chair across the room from Sarah. Exhaustion showed in the dark circles beneath her eyes, but she wouldn't let herself fall asleep, even though they'd been sitting in the sheriff's office for over an hour.

Max, Brody and Sawyer had disappeared down the hallway shortly after they'd arrived. Sawyer had merely told Sarah to stay put.

So she had. She'd stayed, and she'd fretted, and she'd fumed and then fretted some more and watched the clock on the wall slowly tick past midnight. Across the room from them, the dispatcher, Pamela, was doing a decent job of not looking too curious as she answered an occasional call and paged through a magazine.

Sarah was on the verge of going down that hallway beyond Pamela and finding her uncle herself when the blinds over the front door swayed and it opened.

Her uncle, Tristan, entered.

He took one look at her and frowned, but there was no surprise in his expression. "Well." he stopped in front of her, and the overhead light picked out a few silver hairs among his deep gold hair. "Seems there's more going on under my nose than I knew about."

She stood. "Tristan, what's happening? What's Max doing?" She hadn't forgotten Brody's implication that she could reach Coleman Black via her uncle.

He gave Megan a sidelong look. She'd folded her arms around herself and was not looking at anyone. She'd even stopped responding to Sarah's efforts at conversation.

"Pamela—you can keep an eye on Megan?"

The woman nodded at Tristan. She sent a smile in Megan's direction.

It wasn't returned, and Sarah's stomach tightened. She badly wanted to get the girl out of there.

Tristan took Sarah's arm. "Come with me."

She thought, at first, that he was taking her back to the office where Max had disappeared. Instead, he ushered her into an empty office and closed the door.

He gave her a long look and seemed to sigh. “Sit down, Sarah.”

“I don’t want to sit. I want to know *what* is going on.” She wanted to see Max. Not that she knew what she’d say to the man when she did.

He shoved his fingers through his hair. “A damned mess, far as I can tell.” He pulled out one of the two chairs at the scarred Formica-topped table and sat down. “Max’s investigation evidently crossed wires with Brody’s assignment to protect the Devereaux kid.”

She stiffened. “How did you know Megan’s real name?”

His lips twisted. “Because you’re not the only Clay family member that Coleman Black has tapped for Hollins-Winword. He seems to treat this family like his personal garden for growing agents.”

She reached for the other chair, sitting weakly down on it.

“If I’d known what he’d done, I’d have stopped it, though. How long have you been involved?”

“Seven years.” Her voice was faint.

“Someone—say, an aging white-haired guy—just one day strikes up a conversation with you and, says 'Oh by the way, want to be a spy?'"

She jerked. "I'm not a spy." The idea was ludicrous. "I just...set up a safe house here in the area now and then. That's all. And it's perfectly legal."

Tristan's lips twisted. "Your part is," he agreed. "And I'm glad to know that's the extent of your involvement. Because H.W. can tiptoe along some murky lines in the whole *legal* regard."

Her stomach clenched. "If I'm not the first in the family, then who—"

"Jefferson. Daniel. They're both out of it now. Me?" He looked up at the ceiling and sighed faintly. "Let's just say that I'm not always as smart as they are."

"You've been here in Weaver running Cee-Vid my entire life."

"Close enough. You know the computer biz, squirt. Always a way to keep your fingers in pies that most people don't even know exist."

She shook her head, finding the entire situation unfathomable. Jefferson raised horses. And Daniel worked with her father at the C and had built more than half the new houses on the other side of town. "But—"

The door to the office creaked open and Max appeared.

He looked weary as he eyed the older man. "Great. You, too, huh?"

Tristan unfolded himself from the seat. He clapped Max on the shoulder. "Sorry, man. If I'd have known where your investigation was heading, I could have steered you clear of Paine. Saved you some wasted effort. Now, I'm gonna have to fess up to Sawyer that I didn't get out of the game a long time ago when he thought I did."

"Uncle Sawyer knows, too?"

Tristan's lips twitched. "Hell, squirt, he's the big brother of us all. Yeah. He knows." He dropped a kiss on her forehead and knuckled her head like she was ten years old. "Keep your chin up," he murmured. "Sun always rises in the morning." And with that, he left the office.

Alone with Max, Sarah closed her hands over the back of the metal chair. "You really thought that I could be involved with drugs?"

He reached behind himself and pushed the door closed. "What I believed was that you might not *know* what you were involved with," he countered grimly. "Which is why I would have appreciated it if you'd have stopped with the evasions and just told me the bloody truth about your relationship with Paine."

"There is no relationship."

A muscle ticked in his jaw. "Association, then."

"I didn't think there was anything to tell! All he was doing was protecting that little girl. And for heaven's sake, Max. My uncle surely never thought for a minute that I'd be involved in something illegal. Much less drugs!"

"It wasn't your uncle that suspected it, Sarah. It was *my* boss."

She winced. "Sawyer is your boss." But her stomach, that she'd already thought couldn't sink any lower, was seeming to puddle around her ankles.

Max stared at her from across the width of the table. "Sawyer was cooperating with the special DEA task force I'm on."

The width between them was suddenly miles wider than an old-fashioned Formica table.

Her grip on the back of the chair felt slippery. The ticking of yet another industrial-looking clock on the wall sounded loud and distinct. He wasn't only a cop anymore. He was DEA. "You're working undercover again," she realized aloud. Her voice sounded muddy and dull.

He nodded once.

She swallowed, trying to clear the knot in her throat. "Déjà vu, indeed. Only this time, you didn't clue me in to that particular truth." Before, it had been his situation with Jennifer and Eli that he'd kept to himself.

"You haven't exactly been an open book either, darlin'."

"Does anyone besides Sawyer know why you're really here? Before now, I mean."

"No."

That was something, she supposed. She hadn't been the *only* one he'd kept in the dark.

"How'd you get involved with Hollins-Winword, anyway?"

Her palms hurt from pressing so hard against the chair back. She slowly straightened her fingers and let go. "What does it matter?"

He exhaled roughly. "Because, dammit, everything *about* you matters."

"And you sound so happy about that."

He suddenly raised the chair in front of him a foot and slammed it back down on the linoleum floor.

She winced.

He let go of the chair, shoving it against the

table. "What should I *be* happy about, Sarah? The fact that you don't trust me enough to tell me the truth when I ask for it? Or that my one damn lead turns out to be a dead end the size of a mountain?"

"I've never heard anything about drugs being transported through Weaver. I mean, we have the occasional person busted for marijuana, but—"

"—Ten pounds of methamphetamine were found in Montana last month on a truck hauling Double-C cattle. This morning, Jefferson confiscated another ten that he found in a trailer he was sending out."

She swayed. "And you think my *family* is involved?"

"No."

"God. At least there's that."

"Other than the trucks, we couldn't find a link to your family."

Her hands trembled as she pushed back her hair. "Which means that you actually *looked* for a link."

His gaze didn't flinch. "It's my job, Sarah."

Her eyes burned. She pressed her lips together. "And was *I* part of the job, too?"

"No."

She felt like crying. "Where's Brody?"

His lips tightened again. "Making arrangements for Megan."

She suddenly headed for the door.

"Where are you going?"

"Presumably I'm not under arrest?" She barely waited for his annoyed shake of his head. "Then I'm going to tell Brody that I want Megan to go home with me."

He blocked the door, though. "Your concern is admirable, Sarah, but you're not even the girl's teacher. She probably should be placed with someone who's already raising children."

She winced. "I'd be *raising* my child if I hadn't miscarried him." Her voice was thick. "Now *move* away from the door or I swear, Max, the next thing my uncle will be doing is putting me in a cell for assaulting his fake deputy."

Chapter 14

"I'm sorry, Sarah." Brody was inflexible. She'd found him in her uncle's office, sitting behind Sawyer's desk. "You can't take Megan."

"Why not?"

"Because she's already been placed with a perfectly nice family in Quebec."

"*Quebec!* But that's not even in the country."

"I don't make the arrangements."

"Then who does? Coleman Black?"

Brody shook his head. "He doesn't get involved at that level."

"Tristan. He'll help me."

"He can try. But for now, I've got to take her."

She brushed her hands down her face. "This is a nightmare."

"Only because you've lost your objectivity."

"Thanks for the reminder, Brody. That's *ever* so helpful." But her voice was thick with tears as she turned out of the office. Brody followed.

Megan was still in the lobby where she'd been left. At the sight of Sarah, she slipped off the chair, looking small and defenseless. "It's okay, Miss Clay," she whispered. "Mr. Brody's doing what he has to."

The tears Sarah had been fighting slipped past her lashes, burning hot. The sight of Max handing a file over to Pamela didn't help any. She knelt down and put her arms around Megan's thin shoulders.

How quickly she'd let the girl under her skin. "You can call me. Or write."

Megan hugged her back. "I don't think they'll allow that." She stepped back, her chin trembling. "Thank you for my blouse. It's the nicest thing anyone's given me since… since—" She broke off, looking down at her feet.

Brody muttered something under his breath and surprised everyone when he picked Megan up. "Come on, kid, before we're all crying in our soup." He tossed Megan's coat around her shoulders and carried her out of the sheriff's office. Megan's solemn eyes looked over his shoulder. She lifted her fingertips.

And the door closed behind them as they disappeared into the night.

Sarah covered her face.

When arms surrounded her, she turned against Max and let the tears come even though it was *him* who held her.

Maybe because it *was* Max who held her.

His hands smoothed down her back. “I’ll take you home.”

The word just made Sarah cry harder.

He finally let go of her long enough to push a wad of tissues in her hand and wrap her coat around her shoulders pretty much the same way Brody had done with Megan. Then he nudged her outside and into the SUV he’d left parked outside the door.

When he parked behind her house, her tears had slowed, leaving her feeling numb and empty.

Not even the tight-lipped expression he got when he pushed open her unlocked back door made an impression on her. She tossed her coat on the kitchen table and walked through the darkened house, dropping down on her bed.

A moment later, the mattress dipped as Max sat beside her. “Sarah—”

"Go home, Max."

He was silent for a long moment. "The baby was mine." His voice was low.

She pressed her cheek against the pillow. "Yes."

He let out a long sigh. "When did it happen?"

She rolled onto her back, staring up at the ceiling. Once again, narrow swaths of moonlight shined through the tilted blinds. "I was five months along. It was a boy." She looked sideways at him.

In the dim light, she could see a dark gleam in his eyes and it made her ache inside.

When he finally spoke, his voice sounded hollow, rusty. "What happened?"

"Cervical incompetence." The words were clipped. "By the time we knew, it was too late."

"Why didn't you tell me before?"

"When?" She swallowed. "Should I have run up and interrupted your wedding to Jennifer? Or maybe when you showed up here in Weaver, I should have just blurted it out."

He was silent.

She threw her arm over her eyes. She was so tired. "Leandra is the only one who knew."

"Not even your parents?"

"They'd have worried themselves sick."

"That's a parent's right," he said huskily.

Her eyes burned all over again. "Please go, Max. I can't take any more tonight."

He slowly pushed himself to his feet. But he didn't move to the door. Instead, he moved to the foot of the bed and lifted her foot, slowly pulling off her boot. He set it on the floor beside the bed.

She swiped her cheeks.

He pulled off the other boot and set it next to the first.

Then he unfolded the blanket at the end of the bed and slowly drew it over her. His hand shook as he smoothed it over her hair. "I'm sorry. There're so many reasons that I'm sorry."

She should be out of tears, but they still filled her eyes.

He walked to the doorway. Stopped once more and looked back at her. "You wanted the baby?"

"Yes." She closed her eyes.

"I'm sorry," he said again.

But when she opened her eyes again, he was already gone. "I wanted you, too," she whispered.

Max drove back to the sheriff's station. He found Sawyer, looking tired and worn, leaning back in his chair behind his desk. The man's eyes tracked his entrance and watched silently as Max dropped the keys to the SUV on the desk, followed by his badge, the sheriff's ID, and his radio.

Then the sheriff eyed the display laying across his desk. "Sure you want to do that?"

Max wasn't sure about much of anything, anymore. "Yeah."

"Shame," Sawyer murmured. "Was hoping you might find a reason to stick around this time."

"Think I've done enough damage."

"Because you followed a lead that didn't pan out?"

It was a gross simplification of all that Max had—and hadn't—done. "The task force will send another special agent. I'll make sure he gets the background checks I was nearly finished with. At least *those* I didn't screw up. Only ones left are *you* and Tommy." He turned and walked out the door.

When daylight rolled around a few hours later, he was still awake, sitting in his mother's kitchen. Bundled in a thick robe as she hobbled into the kitchen without aid of her crutches, Genna stopped short at the sight of him. "I didn't even realize you were here,

Max. I didn't hear your truck come home last night."

He'd walked from the station to his mother's place.

Evidently, he wasn't the only one capable of walking. "Where are your crutches?"

She looked innocent. "In my bedroom. Why?"

"Thought you couldn't manage without them."

She tossed up her hands. "Eh, what can I say?" She sat down at the table across from him. "So I'm healing better than I let on. I'm not so feeble as you thought."

"I never thought you were feeble."

Her eyebrows lifted. "And now you know for certain I'm not." She lifted her hands. "What can I say? After more than twenty years, I wanted my family here with me for a while."

"We can't stay, though, Ma. Eli and I will be leaving."

Her lips tightened. "You disappoint me, Massimo."

He exhaled. "Get in line. Coming here was a mistake. I knew it and I came anyway."

"Because you thought I needed you?"

"Something wrong with that? Just come away with us. Back to California. You can live with us or I'll find you a place of your own. Whatever you want. To this day I don't understand why you want to stay in Weaver after what happened here."

She just shook her dark head. "What I want is for my son to stop running from *his* home."

His lips twisted. "So I'm more like Dad than either of us like to admit."

"Oh, *now* you mention your father? You go for years never mentioning his name as if *you* have something to be ashamed of, rather than him." She reached across the table and as if he were still twelve and guilty of cow-tipping, closed his chin in her surprisingly strong fingers. "What happened tonight?"

"I screwed up."

She stared into his face, then sat back in her seat. "Then make it right. You're *not* your father, Max. He never once wanted to really make things right."

"He abandoned us."

She tsked. "Tony would've come back here in a second if I'd have let him. But why would I let him? He betrayed us. I know you thought the sun rose and set on his head. But he lied, he cheated, he stole. Getting caught like he did was just the last straw and I finally found some backbone to make him stay away. Something I *should* have done long before things got so bad. He was no husband and no father I wanted raising you."

"I was practically grown by the time he was sent up."

"You were fifteen," she dismissed. "A baby." She tapped her hand on the table. "So...did you lie? Cheat? Steal? Did you do all these things deliberately, not caring who you harmed? Of course you didn't. You're a grown man, Massimo. You don't want to be like your father, then you don't be like him. You think you messed up, you make it right."

"Some things can't be made right, Ma."

"So you face it and you apologize and you move forward." She shook her head again, her voice tart, but her eyes were as soft as they'd always been. "Your whole life you've been making things right for other people. You're forty years old now. It's time to start making things right for you. Sarah loves you. Stay. Don't give up."

"I didn't say anything about Sarah, Ma."

"You don't have to. I've seen your eyes when you look at her. You never looked at anyone else that way. And I've seen her face when she talks of you. Why do you think I haven't boxed your ears for having your truck parked outside her house at all hours?"

He felt his face flush. Trust a mother to

make a guy want to hang his head even more than it was already hanging. "Little old for ear-boxing," he said.

She just eyed him. "Want to test that theory?"

Amazingly, after the miserable night, the miserable day, the miserable years, he felt a smile tug his lips. He pushed out of the seat, feeling stiff from sitting there so long. He pressed a kiss to her forehead and headed from the room. "Think I'll pass."

"I knew I raised a smart boy."

Upstairs, Max looked in on Eli. He was sleeping face down on the mattress, one foot stuck out from beneath the quilt. Max pulled up the quilt and tucked it over his son's toes.

Eli mumbled and stuck his foot right back out, like it was searching for freedom. He rolled over and blinked blearily. "Am I late for school?"

Max sat down, nudging the boy over. "It's Sunday."

That seemed an even worse fate than it being a school day. "Grandma's gonna make me go to church."

"There are worse things." He eyed his boy. He was so much like Jennifer. "How would you feel if we *didn't* go back to California?"

Eli squinted. "Ever?"

"Not forever. We'd visit Grandma Helene, of course."

"You wanna live here? For good? Are you gonna marry Sarah? 'Cause she's my teacher, you know, and that's well—it might be kinda gross."

Max was pretty sure that marrying Sarah wouldn't be the foregone conclusion that Eli seemed to think.

"What makes you think I want to marry her?"

"'Cause you're all kissy with her. Grandma says you're in love."

Max jerked a little. "She does, huh? It, uh, doesn't mean I didn't love your mom."

'I know. Grandma says that, too."

Grandma says a lot, Max thought.

"So, would that really bother you? If Sarah were…in our lives?"

Eli rolled back over onto his face. "If it keeps her from making me stand next to Chrissy Tanner in the pageant, I guess it's okay."

It was about the last thing in the world that Sarah wanted to do that morning, but she dragged herself into the shower, dried her hair and slapped on enough makeup to hide the circles under her eyes, pulled on a knitted tube of a dress, and took herself to church.

If she didn't, she knew her parents would just come calling afterward to find out why she hadn't joined them as she usually did.

She would have driven, but her car was still parked at the sheriff's station. So, she pulled on her low-heeled leather boots and walked.

They were singing the first hymn when she finally got there, and she pulled off her coat and slipped through the narthex doors, quietly sliding into the pew beside her parents. Her mother gave her a glance, then a second sharper one, before she handed over the opened hymnal she'd been holding.

Sarah stared hard at the page, and tried to pretend she was unaware of her mother's eagle-eyed once-over. By the time the service ended nearly an hour later, she thought she might have passed Jaimie's muster. But as they all filed out of the sanctuary, Sarah felt a finger latch in the back of her collar.

"Not so fast, honey," Jaimie said. She had a smile on her face as she nodded and greeted everyone around them—more than a few of whom were part of the family. She even urged Sarah's father on ahead. "We'll be along in a minute, Matthew."

But Sarah didn't mistake the look in her mother's eyes for casual interest.

Jaimie waited until their pew was empty,

before she spoke. Even then she kept her voice low. "I had an interesting conversation with Darla Rasmussen this morning. Why do I have to hear from her that you spent hours at the sheriff's station last night?"

"Pamela Rasmussen better learn to keep her mouth shut around her mother or Sawyer's going to put her out of her job."

"Don't hedge, Sarah."

She tugged down the close-fitting sleeves of her dress. "It was all a misunderstanding, okay? I accidentally got in the middle of an investigation of Max's."

"Mmm. Well, I can imagine what investigation that is, given what your father has told me. So if it was all a misunderstanding, why do you have circles under your eyes that even I could back a pickup truck into?" It was well known that Jaimie didn't have the best of judgment when it came to driving pickups.

"I'm just tired. After the sale yesterday." *Was it only yesterday?* "And the week I've got coming up with the pageant. It's always busy this time of year for me."

"Sarah!" Eli was weaving his way through the departing people like a salmon going upstream. He finally stopped next to her, and seemed to be vibrating with energy. Maybe that was why his shirt was half untucked, and he had a cowlick standing up at the back of his head. "I can call you that now, right?" He shot Jaimie a look. "Oh, hi, Mrs. Clay."

Jaimie's lips twitched. "Hello, Eli."

"Where's your grandma?"

He looked back at Sarah. "She's out there talking to *everybody*. I don't know how come. We see them every week."

Jaimie covered her mouth, hiding her chuckle. She shot Sarah a look though, one that said their discussion wasn't finished. "I'll leave you in Mr. Scalise's fine hands, here, Sarah."

Eli grinned and held up his palms. "They're even clean."

Despite herself, Sarah smiled. She sat on the wooden arm of the pew and watched her mother walk away. "Didn't want to come to church, huh?"

Eli shook his head fervently. "Well, it's okay once we're here. But I had to get up early and everything."

Sarah nibbled the inside of her lip. "I-is your dad here, too?" She would surely have known if Max had been present in the church.

Eli shook his head. "He's at the office. So, do I get to call you Sarah? All the guys in class are gonna be *so* ticked."

It ought to have alarmed her some to see how much he relished the idea.

But Eli was nothing if not an energizing factor in the classroom. And no matter what had happened between his father and her, she was crazy about the kid. "Well, I think Miss Clay will still be good in the classroom," she said. "But, yes, you may call me Sarah in private."

He gave a choking laugh. "That's a good one." His head swiveled when he heard his name being called. "That's Grandma. Gotta go." He darted off again, his shirttail flapping.

Sarah pressed her hands to her stomach. She had no objectivity where Elijah Scalise was concerned, either.

The church was nearly empty. She picked up her coat and pulled it on, and headed out the rear door rather than facing the gauntlet of people standing around out front drinking their hot coffee while they critiqued the worship service and traded gossip.

Walking back home didn't take long, and she went in through the kitchen, only to stop short at the sight of Max sitting at her kitchen table.

She slowly unwound her scarf, trying to

will her heart back into some normal rhythm. "What are you doing here?"

"Proving what happens when you don't lock your doors. Anyone can get in."

She slid out of her coat. She didn't want to recognize that he looked even more tired than she had before she'd used up half a tube of concealer. "Taking your deputy duties a little seriously, aren't you? Oh, that's right. You're not really a deputy."

"I'm a deputy all right." He pulled out his badge and flipped it on the table. "What I'm not is a special agent with the DEA. I resigned this morning."

She stared at the badge on the table. It reflected the sunlight coming from the window, seeming to wink up at her. "Why?"

"Because we're staying in Weaver. Eli and me."

Her coat was a bundle against her waist as she hugged it to herself. "So that's what he was going on about at church."

Max's gaze sharpened. "You saw him?"

"I saw half the town," she countered. "Or so it seemed."

"What'd he say?"

"He wanted to know if he could call me Sarah from now on."

"That's *all* he said?"

Sarah lifted her shoulders. "Pretty much. What else should he have said?"

"Nothing." He pushed to his feet, looking oddly restless. "I just wanted to tell you. That we're not leaving Weaver."

"Okay."

"Just like that…okay."

She wasn't sure how long she could keep up the façade. "What else do you want me to say? You're staying. For now. I get it."

"Not *for now*. For good."

The knot in her chest felt like it was choking her. Slowly. Painfully. "Right."

He exhaled. "You don't believe me."

"You're not going to be happy being a deputy for long."

"Maybe I won't be. Maybe I'll be the sheriff, and serve out a term that's as long as Sawyer's has been."

"You won't win if you run against him."

"I will win, because he'll be the one telling the voters to elect me."

Beneath cover of the coat, her fingernails dug into her palms. "What about your case? The trafficking case?"

"It's still open. I'll just be on the local side of the investigation now."

She pressed her lips together. "Why now?"

"Don't you know?" He stopped in front of

her. Tucked his knuckles under her chin and nudged her face upward. "Because Weaver is where *you* are."

She swallowed with an effort. "I don't need you feeling sorry for me, Max."

"That's good, because I don't." His thumb brushed over her cheek. "I feel sorry about *everything* that's happened. But you're talking about pity. And that I don't feel. Except maybe for Chrissy Tanner because Eli definitely has a bee in his bonnet when it comes to her." His half-hearted attempt at humor died. "I'm sorry for what you lost. I'm sorry that I didn't even know what we'd lost, until now. I'm sorry that I wasn't there for you. But I'm here now. And I'm not going anywhere again. Not unless I have to follow you somewhere else. And I will."

Her knees felt weak. "The past is over, Max. You don't have to do this, trying to make up for it. It's done."

"There's no way I can make up for what happened in the past," he said quietly. "And maybe it's done, but neither one of us will ever forget it happened. Maybe you'll understand in time that I would have cut off my arm to keep from hurting you as badly as I did. But my staying here now isn't about what happened then. It's about us. Now. Here." He lowered his head, brushing his lips over hers. Softly. Gently.

She shuddered, steeling herself against him. Against letting herself believe.

Before, she'd barely comprehended how much she could love this man, and her heart had been shattered.

Now, she did comprehend it. She knew, truly knew, what kind of man he was. The depth of caring that he possessed. She knew, and she loved him all the more for it.

And she knew that when he moved on, this time it would destroy her.

"It's about us from here on out," he said softly. "I love you, Sarah. I want to spend my life with you." He dragged the coat out from between them and closed his warm hands over her cold ones. "Will you marry me?"

She bit her lip. Looked into the eyes that were brown and green and so beautiful they made her want to weep.

She slowly pulled her hands free.

"I'm sorry, Max. But…no."

His skin paled. He stepped back, shoving his hands in the front pockets of his jeans. "I can't say I blame you," he said evenly.

She looked away, dashing her hand over her face.

"I don't want to make you cry, Sarah. I never wanted that."

"I know." She pressed her hands to her stomach. "I…just… I need you to—"

"Sshh." He reached out and thumbed away another tear from her cheek. "I know. I'll go."

And a moment later, he did.

She watched him close the kitchen door after himself. Heard his boots walk down the steps.

She moved to the door and slowly turned the lock.

And then she sat down, her back against the door, and wept.

Chapter 15

The badge sat on her table for hours.

She knew it was there when she finally dragged herself off the floor of her kitchen and went into the bathroom to soak her face.

She knew it was there when she changed out of her dress and pulled on the oldest, warmest, softest sweater and jeans that she possessed.

She particularly knew it was there when she sat down and clutched it in her hand until the engraving on it made a dent in her palm.

Sooner or later, Max would need it, if only to turn in to Sawyer when he changed his mind about staying in Weaver.

She tucked it in her pocket, found her wallet and let herself out of the house. The afternoon was brilliant and cold, the promise of snow tickling at her nose. She walked downtown and headed to the sheriff's office. She'd leave the badge for Max with the dispatcher, pick up her car and go back home.

Simple steps seemed all she could manage.

There was only one cruiser parked beside the office when she got there. Her car was still sitting where she'd left it in the lot. If she'd had her wits about her, she would have just picked it up after she'd left the church earlier that day.

But wits seemed in short supply these days.

She pushed open the door. The blinds on the back of the window swayed as it swung closed behind her. "I need to drop this off..." Her voice trailed off. The badge she'd pulled from her pocket slipped loosely out of her hand.

Max and Pamela Rasmussen were standing against the wall facing Tommy Potter.

Tommy Potter who held a gun in his hand.

Sarah's shocked gaze met Max's.

"Get over there." Tommy gestured with his gun. "With them."

Sarah couldn't have uttered a word to save her soul. She slowly crossed the room, giving the deputy a wide berth. Pamela was crying softly. She grabbed Sarah's hand in a death grip.

"Locked doors," Max murmured.

"Shut up." Tommy reached behind him, though, and flipped the lock on the office door.

"What do you think you're gonna accomplish, Tommy? Let the women go." Max's voice was calm.

The deputy looked harried. "I need the product from the trailer. Tell me where it is, and I'll be outta here."

"Call it what it really is, man," Max said. "It's meth. It's what's going to work its way into the schools here. It's what's going to start killing kids and adults. Anyone who's not strong enough to say no when it's suddenly so easily available. Because of people like you."

"I'm not like that!" He lifted his gun and dashed his hand over his forehead, but sweat still gleamed there. "We're not getting rid of it here."

"Just dumping it on some other unsuspecting, vulnerable town."

"It's a lot of money. You think a guy can get ahead on a deputy salary?" His laugh was short and harsh and horribly, horribly sad. "There's no woman here who'd live on that."

Max slowly took a step forward. Tommy didn't seem to notice, but Sarah tightened her grip on Pamela's hand. The other woman squeezed back. Her shoulder was pressed against Sarah's and she could feel her shaking.

Or maybe it was Sarah who was shaking. Twice now in less than two days, she'd seen guns waving around.

Only then, it had been Max and Brody, both of whom she'd trusted not to lose their heads while she'd stood between them.

Tommy? She would never have believed it of him if she weren't witnessing it with her own eyes. He'd been in Weaver for *years*. Always quiet around women, she'd *thought* he was a decent guy. *Everyone* thought he was a decent guy. But there was no question. He wielded that gun as if he were fully prepared to use it.

"So this is *really* about a girl? Who? Dude, if she doesn't know what a catch you are on a deputy's salary, what would you want with her anyway? Plenty of fish in the sea."

Tommy snorted. "Yeah. You'd say that. You're screwing the Untouchable Teach." His gaze cut to Sarah for a moment.

She swallowed, pressing her lips together. From the corner of her vision, she saw Max's hands fist and just as abruptly uncurl. "And

I'm doing it on a deputy's salary," he said. "Hell, Tommy. You're ten years younger 'n me and in a helluva lot better shape. All you'd have to do is crook your finger and Dee Crowder would come running."

Tommy was evidently tired of the topic. He leveled the gun at Max. "You have another salary and everyone in this town knows it now, thanks to motormouth there." He jerked his chin toward Pamela.

"You're calling me a gossip? Oh, that's rich coming from *you*." Pamela bit her lip, and went silent when Max gave her a sideways look.

"Where's the package?" Tommy demanded. "I know Jefferson turned it in here. Sawyer told me."

Max slowly lifted his hands, and shook his head. "If I knew, don't you think I'd tell you just so you'd put that gun away? The sheriff handled it himself. Why don't we call him and ask."

"You're a regular laugh factory," Tommy said. He gestured with the gun. "Everybody go. Into Sawyer's office."

Pamela kept her death grip on Sarah's hand. Max turned, giving them an almost imperceptible nod. Sarah felt like her heart was going to explode out of her chest. She and Pamela turned and started walking toward the dispatcher's desk. They had to pass it before they could reach Sawyer's office beyond it.

As they neared the desk, Pamela stumbled, knocking into Sarah. Her hip hit the desk.

"What are you trying to pull?" Tommy's voice was loud. "Move it."

"I'm sorry!" Pamela had started crying again. Soft, frightened snuffles.

"Get some backbone," Tommy snapped.

Sarah turned her head and glared at the man. "I never realized you were a jerk," she snapped. "I'm glad now that I never went out with you when you asked."

Max's eyes looked like murky pools of green water. He shook his head sharply.

"Shut up," Tommy ordered.

Sarah turned. She and Pamela passed the desk, Max crowding closely behind them.

They entered Sawyer's office. Tommy stood in the doorway, blocking their exit. "Open every drawer," he said flatly. "Every cabinet."

"Most of them are locked," Max pointed out.

Tommy swore. "Open…every…one."

Max shrugged. He nodded toward the filing cabinet in the far corner of the room. "Sarah, you try there. Sawyer keeps his key to it in the top drawer of his desk. Pam, check the desk drawers."

"Glad you're being helpful," Tommy said snidely.

Sarah fumbled open the top drawer. There was a metal key ring inside holding a few small keys. She pulled it out and turned toward the filing cabinet. Pamela was yanking at the other drawers of the desk.

Max had flipped back the cupboard door on the wall that hid the locking safe. "Afraid I failed safecracking at the academy."

Tommy muttered an oath. He strode over to Sarah, snatching the keys out of her hand. He shoved them at Max. "Try these."

Max just looked at the keys. "Tommy, it's a combination lock. It doesn't take a key. Look for yourself."

The deputy shoved Pamela out of his way. The woman stumbled again, falling against the desk. Sarah caught her, trying to steady her. Tommy gestured at Max. "Move."

Max shifted. Tommy moved closer to see around the cupboard door. "That's not a comb—"

Max slammed the cupboard door in Tommy's face.

Pamela cried out.

Sarah froze.

Tommy fell back, grunting. But he swung around in a crouch and went at Max.

The two men crashed to the floor, knocking wildly into the two chairs in front of Sawyer's. Sarah shoved at Pam. "Go. Call help."

"But—"

"Go!" She grabbed the letter opener she'd managed to palm when they'd first knocked into Pamela's desk. But the two men were wrestling, arms locked in terrifying battle and Sarah didn't know *what* to do. She should have used the opener on Tommy when he'd grabbed the keys—

"Get out," Max said through gritted teeth. He sent his elbow into Tommy's jaw.

"I'm not leaving you!"

"*Now* you say that." His head snapped back as Tommy's fist caught him, and Sarah cried out as the men rolled again, this time with Tommy on top.

She grabbed the desk chair that was blocking her way to the door and smashed it over Tommy's back. The wood splintered. He swore violently and turned on her, snatching her ankle, yanking her off her feet.

Max latched his arms around Tommy's neck. "One…more…move," he said, breathing hard. "Come on, Tommy. Give me a reason."

Sarah scrambled back, pulling her legs out

of Tommy's reach. But the deputy was scrabbling at the arm cutting off his oxygen.

She snatched up the gun that he'd finally dropped, and pushed to her feet, holding it between both hands. "Enough!"

Max didn't respond. Tommy's face was brilliant red.

"Max, please. Stop."

Slowly, infinitesimally, she saw him begin to relax his hold.

Tommy sagged, sucking in gulping breaths.

Max shoved him onto the ground and came over to Sarah, lifting the gun carefully out of her tight grip. "It's okay. Everything's okay now." He worked the gun loose.

From outside in the lobby, they could hear commotion.

But Tommy was finally too spent to fight anymore.

Sawyer appeared in the office doorway, tight-lipped. His blue eyes traveled over Sarah. "You okay?"

She nodded, hugging her arms around herself.

His gaze slid to Max. There was a cut near his eye, and a trickle of blood was working its way down his chin. "Peaceful town you got here, Sheriff," he said, and handed over Tommy's weapon to the man.

Then he went over to Tommy and pulled the cuffs off the man's belt and clipped them around his wrists. "Get up, you miserable puke."

Dave Ruiz, the other deputy, had appeared, too. "If I weren't seeing this with my own eyes, I wouldn't have believed it when the sheriff filled me in." He took Tommy's arm from Max. "I'll put him in lockup." He led the disgraced deputy away.

Sawyer eyed the chaotic office. "I'm finally losing my taste for this. When a man you thought you knew could go so off track—" He shook his head. "Good thing you'll be taking over soon, Max."

Sarah's lips parted.

Sawyer eyed them both. "We can do the paperwork on this tomorrow."

Max nodded. "Fine with me." His voice was weary.

"One question, though." Sawyer eyed him. "What were you even doing here, today? Thought you were off."

"I was. But Tommy bugging us about changing shifts kept niggling at me. Dave told me he'd kept on him about it until he finally gave in and switched. I wanted to know why Tommy was so anxious to be on duty today."

Sawyer frowned. "He was after the stuff

that *you* had me announce was here. Could have let me know which fish you were baiting, son."

"After the mess with Paine, I wasn't sure I trusted my own hunch. Didn't expect you to. I definitely didn't expect visitors." He slanted Sarah a look.

Sawyer sighed. "Maybe we've all been a little shortsighted. If I'd seen what Tommy was up to sooner..."

"Not every case is perfect," Max said.

Sarah knew he was thinking of E.J. "So if the package of drugs isn't *here*, where is it?"

"The field office has already taken it," Max said.

"Along with your resignation," Sawyer added. He shook his head. "Ironic timing." He stepped out of the office. "Pam won't be back, I'll bet. Gonna need *another* dispatcher." He tilted back his head. Smiled faintly. "That'll be *your* headache, Max. Now go on. Let Sarah mop you up."

Max's gaze slanted toward Sarah. "She's not in the mopping business, I'm afraid." He went out into the lobby area, his movements stiff.

Sarah chewed the inside of her lip as she followed him. "Wait."

Max stopped. He sent her a look that had

her heart aching. She was barely aware of Sawyer quietly disappearing back into his office where he closed the door.

"You don't have to, Sarah. I'm capable of cleaning up my own wounds."

She pressed her palms together and slowly walked toward him. "I'm afraid I do have to help." She knelt down and picked up his badge that she'd dropped when she'd come in. She opened her palm and held it up to him. "Because I don't think I can heal *my* wounds if I let you walk away."

She looked up at him. Frowned at the cuts on his face. "I thought it would hurt more if I let you back in here—" she touched her chest over her charging heartbeat "—and you left again. But—but seeing you with Tommy like that, I knew that I couldn't wait around for that day to happen—for that day when you walked away." Her eyes flooded with tears. "He could have shot you. Right then and there. I'd have lost you without ever having been *with* you. I don't want that to happen, Max. I love you. And if I haven't already ruined—"

He caught her face in his hands and covered her mouth with his.

She opened her mouth to him, and he swallowed her soft cry. "I love you," she said against him.

He circled his arms around her and pulled her closer. "Don't ever stop."

She shook her head. Slid her arms around his shoulders and held on.

For life.

Epilogue

"Merry Christmas, Mrs. Scalise."

Sarah looked up from the photo album on her lap as Max came into the room.

They'd gotten married only a week before. A small affair, held in the living room at the Double-C, with just their immediate family and a few friends.

Sarah had worn her mother's wedding gown and Max had been in his dress uniform. Eli had been best man, and though he'd dropped the ring, he'd quickly found it. Leandra had been matron of honor and had laughed that Sarah had taken her "simple" wedding advice seriously.

It had been quickly put together and beautiful and far more perfect than any elaborate wedding Sarah might have dreamed up as a girl.

Now, they were staying with Genna, at least until her cast came off in a few weeks. Beyond that, they hadn't yet determined where they would end up living.

Her house was comfortable enough for two, but with Eli, they would definitely be tight. Unfortunately, moving out to one of the newer houses on the far side of town held little appeal for any of them.

Now, she was just happy where they were. She smiled up at him. "Merry Christmas, Sheriff." The speed at which Sawyer had resigned had been daunting. Max had been appointed acting sheriff until the special election was held in January and he could officially be voted into office.

He moved next to her and she ran her hand up his leg. He laughed softly and bent down to sit beside her on the soft rug. He wore dark blue pajama bottoms in deference to the other people in the house, and a terrycloth robe that hung loose from his wide shoulders. "Couldn't sleep, or did you come down here to rattle a few packages?"

Behind them, the fire that she'd started

when she'd come downstairs was beginning to catch. It crackled softly.

"I had a few things to deliver on Santa's behalf," she said.

He looked over at the fireplace. The stocking that Eli had hung was bulging with little gifts. "Santa's been busy," he murmured, smiling faintly, because the stocking looked even fuller than it had when *he'd* delivered a few things, too. "What're you looking at?"

She lifted the album that Genna had given her the evening before as a gift. "You were such a pretty boy, Max."

"Exactly what every *man* wants to hear," he drawled. He reached over and angled the book on her lap so he could see. "God. Those *are* old pictures. What did my mother do? Raid the storage boxes in the attic or something?"

"I love this album," Sarah said, smiling and holding it protectively to her bosom.

"Sentimental woman," he accused, but his lips were curving. He ran his palm up her spine. "You know, it'll probably be another hour, at least, before Eli shows his face. Even on a Christmas morning that kid hasn't made it up before dawn."

"Shocking." Sarah leaned back against him and sighed as his hand drifted over her shoulder, grazing her breast through her robe. "Derek and I were *always* up before the sun. Dad always complained that he wished we were so perky during the rest of the year when there were chores to be done."

"Yeah, well, be grateful for small mercies." Max's lips nibbled at the nape of her neck and shivers danced down her spine. "It's hard enough finding a few minutes alone to make love to my bride." He reached around her and pulled the album from her loose grasp, then slowly nudged her down onto the rug.

She smiled, looking up into his eyes. "I have a Christmas gift for you."

His lips curved. His eyes were heavy-lidded and full of intent. "My favorite kind of gift," he assured.

She laughed softly. "Well, there's that, too."

He propped his elbow beside her head and slowly drew his fingers through her hair, spreading it around her head. "Do I get to unwrap it?"

"Not for another eight months or so."

He froze. "What?"

She squelched the quick dart of nervousness accosting her. "I know we haven't talked about it yet or anything."

"You're pregnant?"

She slowly nodded. "I… I got up early this morning and did a home test thing."

"You know this early?"

"The lines turned bright pink. According to the directions, you get false negatives, but not false positives."

His gaze was turning decidedly worried. "What about what happened before?"

She slid her hands around his neck. "Now that I *know* about the problem, they can take measures to prevent a miscarriage. I talked with Rebecca about it last week when I started to suspect. I might have to be off my feet for a while somewhere along the way, but there's no reason I can't carry our baby to term."

"And you're happy about it?" His eyes searched her face.

She drew his head closer. "Most definitely." She lifted her head and brushed her lips over his. He deepened the kiss for a moment that was entirely too brief before he was lifting his head again.

She made a protesting sound.

"We're *really* going to need a bigger house," he said.

She laughed softly. "We'll figure it out. My uncle Daniel can *build* us a house. Another bedroom is no big deal." She leaned up to catch his lips once more. Her legs moved restlessly against his.

He closed his hands over her shoulders, gently pinning her to the rug. “Another two bedrooms,” he said.

“Well, one for Eli. One for the baby. So two bedrooms. Besides ours, of course.” She drew her foot along his calf.

“One for Eli. One for the baby.” His hand swept gently down over her abdomen, his expression a combination of awe and possession that she would carry with her for the rest of her days. “And one for Megan.”

She blinked. “What?” The words sank in a little more fully. She scrambled from beneath him, pushing him down onto the rug and peering into his face. “Megan?” She’d talked to Tristan a half-dozen times but her uncle had never once indicated he’d have any sway with her placement.

“Here.” He fumbled in his robe and pulled an envelope out of his pocket. “It came yesterday. You and Ma were in the kitchen cooking.”

She took the envelope and pulled out the single sheet inside. “It’s a telegram from Coleman Black.” She frowned, shooting Max a look. “And it’s addressed to *you.* You’re not keeping any secrets about Hollins-Winword from me, are you?”

He snorted softly. “Think there’re enough folks in your family involved with them. I’ll stick to sheriffing, thanks.”

“Then how did you reach him? Tristan kept telling me there wasn’t anything he could do.”

“You just didn’t go to enough uncles, darling. Between Daniel and Jefferson, they managed to pull some magic with the guy. Evidently, he had a lot to do with your cousin Angeline making it into the country when she was a child, and helping get through the red tape of Maggie and Daniel adopting her.”

Sarah focused on the telegram again, but it was hard to read when her hand was shaking. “She’s going to be here by New Year’s Day.” She cast a look at Max. “What if she doesn’t *want* to live with us? What if Eli doesn’t want her here?”

He pushed his fingers through her hair. “She will,” he promised. “He will.”

Sarah looked into his eyes and saw nothing but the future written there.

It wouldn’t all be smooth sailing, she knew.

What was?

But she knew that whatever their lives brought, they’d meet it all, together. “I love you, Max.”

He smiled slowly and drew her down with him. “I love you, too.”

* * *

On the stairs above them, Genna Scalise smiled softly, looked to the heavens and gave a silent prayer. Then she quietly thumped her way back to bed.

She didn't *have* to get up and start breakfast just yet…

* * * * *

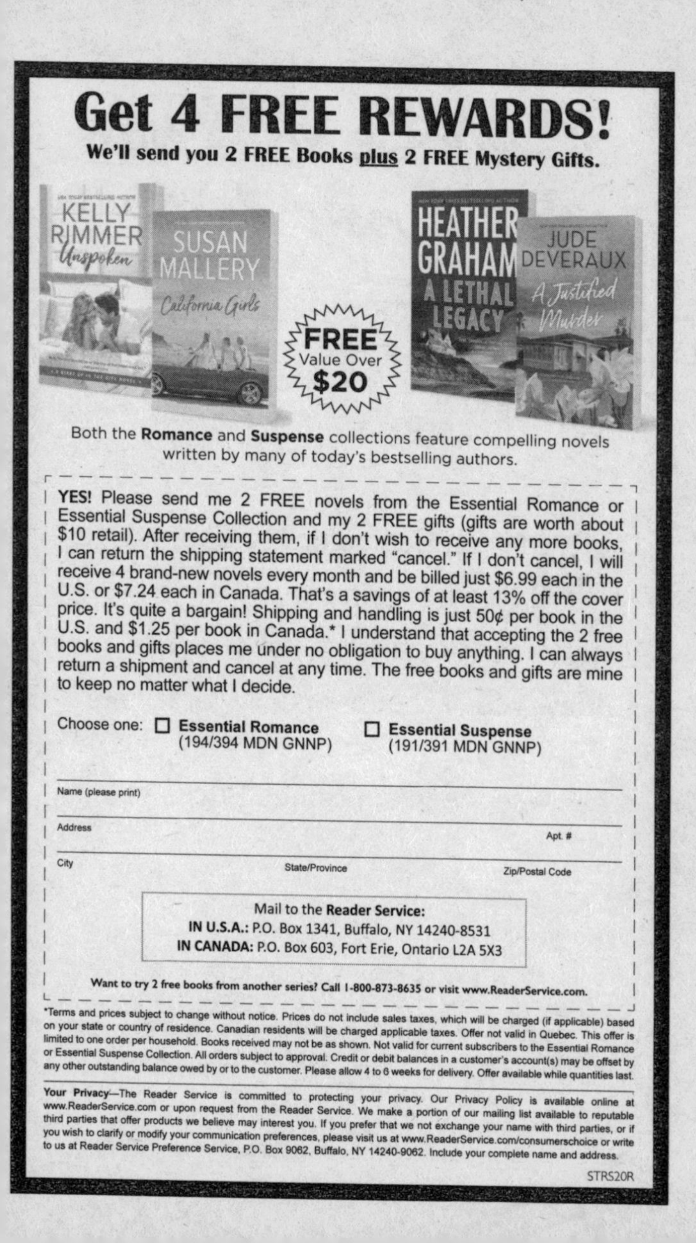
Get 4 FREE REWARDS!
We'll send you 2 FREE Books plus 2 FREE Mystery Gifts.
KELLY RIMMER
Unspoken
SUSAN MALLERY
California Girls
FREE
Value Over
$20
HEATHER GRAHAM
A LETHAL LEGACY
JUDE DEVERAUX
A Justified Murder
Both the Romance and Suspense collections feature compelling novels written by many of today's bestselling authors.
YES! Please send me 2 FREE novels from the Essential Romance or Essential Suspense Collection and my 2 FREE gifts (gifts are worth about $10 retail). After receiving them, if I don't wish to receive any more books, I can return the shipping statement marked "cancel." If I don't cancel, I will receive 4 brand-new novels every month and be billed just $6.99 each in the U.S. or $7.24 each in Canada. That's a savings of at least 13% off the cover price. It's quite a bargain! Shipping and handling is just 50¢ per book in the U.S. and $1.25 per book in Canada.* I understand that accepting the 2 free books and gifts places me under no obligation to buy anything. I can always return a shipment and cancel at any time. The free books and gifts are mine to keep no matter what I decide.
Choose one: ☐ Essential Romance (194/394 MDN GNNP) ☐ Essential Suspense (191/391 MDN GNNP)
Name (please print)
Address
Apt. #
City
State/Province
Zip/Postal Code
Mail to the Reader Service:
IN U.S.A.: P.O. Box 1341, Buffalo, NY 14240-8531
IN CANADA: P.O. Box 603, Fort Erie, Ontario L2A 5X3
Want to try 2 free books from another series? Call 1-800-873-8635 or visit www.ReaderService.com.
*Terms and prices subject to change without notice. Prices do not include sales taxes, which will be charged (if applicable) based on your state or country of residence. Canadian residents will be charged applicable taxes. Offer not valid in Quebec. This offer is limited to one order per household. Books received may not be as shown. Not valid for current subscribers to the Essential Romance or Essential Suspense Collection. All orders subject to approval. Credit or debit balances in a customer's account(s) may be offset by any other outstanding balance owed by or to the customer. Please allow 4 to 6 weeks for delivery. Offer available while quantities last.
Your Privacy—The Reader Service is committed to protecting your privacy. Our Privacy Policy is available online at www.ReaderService.com or upon request from the Reader Service. We make a portion of our mailing list available to reputable third parties that offer products we believe may interest you. If you prefer that we not exchange your name with third parties, or if you wish to clarify or modify your communication preferences, please visit us at www.ReaderService.com/consumerschoice or write to us at Reader Service Preference Service, P.O. Box 9062, Buffalo, NY 14240-9062. Include your complete name and address.
STRS20R